This copy of

MYSTERY OF THE
STONE TIGER
by Carolyn Keene

belongs to

_____

_____

Carolyn Keene
Mystery of the Stone Tiger

SPARROW
BOOKS

A Sparrow Book
Published by Arrow Books Limited
17–21 Conway Street, London W1P 5HL

An imprint of the Hutchinson Publishing Group

London Melbourne Sydney Auckland
Johannesburg and agencies
throughout the world

First published in Great Britain 1981
Reprinted 1981

Made and printed in Great Britain
by The Anchor Press Ltd
Tiptree, Essex

ISBN 0 09 926290 8

CONTENTS

CHAPTER I

Haunted Home Town

"Our town haunted!" Louise cried. "A black-robed ghost roaming around!"

Louise and Jean Dana stared at each other, then at their Aunt Harriet, who said, "But that's unbelievable. What else does Cora say in her letter?"

The three Danas, en route home to Oak Falls from a long trip, were in a Chicago hotel room. The two sisters and their aunt had planned to stay for some sightseeing, but this latest news made them wonder if perhaps they should go directly home. They had been away for some time on a Western trip.

Cora Appel, a timid but faithful young woman who came during the day to help Miss Dana with the housework at their Oak Falls home, had sent a special-delivery letter to the hotel.

"I'll read the rest," said Louise, who was an attractive brunette of seventeen.

Pretty, blonde-haired Jean sat on the edge of her chair and listened wide-eyed. The girls' aunt kept her usual composure. But she did not discount the news. "Though Cora *is* inclined to exaggerate," said Miss Dana, "she always bases her stories on truth."

Louise went on reading:

" 'The police are telling everybody to stay off the streets at night. Some awful things have been reported in the newspaper—people chased by the ghost, and a tiger nearly clawed a man in the West Woods.' "

"A tiger—in Oak Falls!" Jean cried out. "What else has happened?"

The letter continued:

" 'I'm afraid to be in this house alone, even in the daytime. Louise and Jean, *please* come home *quick* and solve the mystery!' "

"It does sound pretty spooky," Jean remarked. "What say we let the sightseeing go and rush home?"

"And start working on the mystery," Louise added. "Aunt Harriet, do you mind?"

Miss Dana laughed. "It's just what I'd expect of you two young sleuths. I'll make a bargain with you. We'll phone Cora and try to get more facts. If she or any of our friends is in danger, we'll go."

Jean darted to the phone and put in the call as the other two crowded nearby. Soon Cora answered, "Hello. . . . Yes. . . . Who is it?"

"It's Jean. We just received your letter. What's

the real story on this haunted-town business?"

"Oh, it's true—every bit. Only it's worse'n I told you, really." Cora gave a little scream. "It—it chased me last night!"

"What chased you?"

"That black-robed ghost."

"You mean—"

"It was like this," Cora explained. "I was kind o' late gettin' away from your house, knowin' you'd be home soon, and it was pretty dark when I left. Well, I just got out the kitchen door when it seemed like that ghost came right out o' the bushes and started for me. I ran for dear life. He didn't catch me, but just as I got to the bus station, I was so scared I went blanko. Yes, just blacked right out and woke up in the police station."

"What a shame!" murmured Jean. "You certainly had a fright. Did you get a look at the face of the ghost?"

"Face? That thing's a spirit—they don't have faces," Cora protested. "Oh, it's terrible, terrible! *Please* come home!"

Jean looked towards Aunt Harriet, who nodded. "We'll take the first plane we can get out of here, Cora. See you tomorrow. And you'd better go home soon."

"Oh, I will. And I feel better now. I been tellin' *everybody* how many mysteries you solved, and if you girls would only come back, you'd solve this one!"

"Better not brag about us," Jean said, laughing, as she hung up.

The Dana girls were modest about their sleuthing ability. They had been successful on several occasions in tracking down thieves and impostors. Louise and Jean had become orphans while very young and for many years had lived with their Aunt Harriet and her brother Ned who captained the ocean liner *Balaska*.

The sisters attended Starhurst, a boarding school for girls at Penfield, where they had solved some mysteries. Now they seemed to be confronted with another.

"A ghost and a tiger," Jean murmured.

Louise telephoned the airport and was able to obtain three reservations for a late-afternoon flight. She then called Cora to let her know their arrival time. Supper was served aboard the plane and Jean remarked with a grin, "I'm sure this is better than anything Applecore left in the refrigerator." Jean often used this nickname for Cora, whose last name was Appel.

"Poor girl! I hope she arrived home without any more scares," said Aunt Harriet.

With good weather and a strong tail wind the plane landed that evening ahead of schedule. The Danas deplaned, claimed their luggage, and hailed a taxi. The driver proved to be talkative, and the girls decided to question him about the ghost.

"We've been away for several weeks," said Louise. "Anything new going on in town?"

"I'll say there is," the man answered promptly. "Oak Falls is havin' a sure-enough mystery. Say, lock those doors. I don't want any black-robed ghost climbin' into my cab. One o' our drivers, Tom, had a narrow escape. He'd stopped for a red light on a country crossroad. Suddenly this ghost comes out o' nowhere and gets in the cab.

" 'Keep goin',' it says, 'till I tell you to stop.' Tom was shakin' like an earthquake 'cause he figured his passenger was a nut and might have a gun. He had to drive five miles—past the West Woods —and near died o' heart failure. But the ghost got out near a housin' development and disappeared."

The three Danas looked at one another. So Cora's story was not an exaggeration! Peaceful, lovely, conservative Oak Falls had been invaded by a troublemaker! For what reason?

"Anything else happen?" Louise asked.

"Well, there's the tiger story, but folks are inclined to think that was made up."

"What *is* the story?" Jean prodded.

The taxi driver said that a group of high school boys had gone to West Woods for a picnic and had been confronted by a snarling tiger. They had fled, unharmed. He also mentioned the man that Cora had told them about.

"The police searched the woods, but couldn't

find any tiger," the taximan concluded, "so they think the boys were playin' a joke—and that the man who claimed he was nearly clawed by the tiger just wanted to get his name in the newspaper."

"They haven't admitted it?" Aunt Harriet asked.

"No, ma'am. Those boys and the man stick to their stories, and say they wouldn't go near that woods for a million dollars."

By this time the taxi had reached the side street on which the Danas' big old-fashioned fieldstone house stood.

"Home, sweet— Oh!" cried Aunt Harriet as she gazed from the taxi window at the darkened house.

Quickly the others turned to look. The sisters gasped and the taxi driver gave a startled outcry. *One of the living-room windows glowed with an eerie green light. Peering over the sill was a grotesque, leering face crowned with dishevelled hair!*

Instantly the taximan started to drive away. "You're not goin' in there," he told the Danas. "There's more to that than a trick!"

"I guess you're right," said Aunt Harriet. "But we'll get out, and go to the next house. Friends of ours live there. I'll call the police to investigate."

The man was only too glad to be relieved of any further responsibility. He set the luggage on the walk to the Dana house, took his fare, and sped off.

The Danas' neighbour, Mr. Pyne, answered their ring. He greeted them warmly, and his wife came to the hall and invited them in. But their smiles of welcome turned to looks of alarm when they heard about the strange reception the Danas had encountered.

"I'll call the police," Mr. Pyne offered.

Jean had run to a side window and was gazing at her own house. "I see a moving light inside!" she declared, but by the time the others had reached her, the light was gone.

"Someone *is* in there—maybe a burglar," Mrs. Pyne said nervously.

"But why would he advertise the fact by putting that horrible, gorillalike face in the window?" asked Aunt Harriet.

"To scare us away until he finished looting the place," Jean guessed. "Why don't we go over and stop him?"

"No!" Aunt Harriet said firmly.

In less than ten minutes four policemen arrived. Miss Dana gave them a key to her house, and they hurried over to investigate. Louise and Jean followed but were ordered to remain outside. They watched as light after light was switched on. Finally the officers walked onto the porch.

"No one is in there now," Sergeant Renley reported to the Danas. He was carrying the mask, which he said he would take to headquarters. "Go in the house if you wish. We'll keep an eye on the place during the night. You'll be safe. We've taken off several fingerprints from the window sill and will check them out."

The officer asked the Danas to look around to see if anything had been stolen. They hurriedly checked the silver and jewellery and announced that everything seemed to be intact.

"Then we'll be off," the sergeant said, adding that they had not found a forced means of entry. "The intruder must have gotten a key, somehow. Call us if you need any more help. By the way, when we first came in, the odour of burning incense was very strong. Do you know anything about that?"

"No, but we'll ask our maid when she comes in the morning," said Aunt Harriet. "She was here cleaning today and may have burned some incense."

Louise, who had gone out to the hall, suddenly exclaimed, "This is strange! I wonder when it came."

She walked up to the others, carrying a sealed envelope. On it were printed the words: *Deliver this to your friend Elise Hilary and be sure she reads it to you.*

"How can I do that?" Louise asked. "She's in India."

"Not any longer," Sergeant Renley said. "Perhaps you don't know that her father was killed in India, and she and her mother came back here a couple of weeks ago."

"I *didn't* know. How dreadful!" Louise said.

"Yes, it was a great tragedy. If you want to see your friend, she and her mother still live in the small house on the grounds of the estate. As you know, Mr. Hilary turned the big house into a museum to display his game trophies from India."

"I've heard about the place but have never been there," Louise answered.

As the officer moved towards the front door, Jean said to him, "We've just been told about a mystery in town and a black-robed ghost and other strange happenings. When did this start?"

Sergeant Renley frowned as if embarrassed by a touchy question, but said, "I can't give you the exact date, but it all began shortly after the Hilarys' return—about the time that the stone tiger was delivered to the Hilary Museum."

CHAPTER II

A Frightening Jolt

"A STONE tiger delivered to the museum?" Louise repeated. "Please tell us about it."

Sergeant Renley said it had been a gift to Mr. Hilary from a maharajah in India.

"I understand Mr. Hilary saved one of the maharajah's villages from a man-eating tiger and the gift was given in gratitude for that. Unfortunately he didn't live to see the gift or have time to tell his family about it."

"How sad!" Aunt Harriet spoke up. "Well, the fine museum here is a tribute to Mr. Hilary's memory. It is supported by an admission fee, I believe."

"Yes, and Mrs. Hilary and her daughter have put some of the money they inherited into it. Since the scare here in town, people haven't been going to see the exhibits, and, of course, the curator's salary has to be paid."

"Why are people staying away?" Jean asked.

Sergeant Renley said that the townspeople had come to the police with all kinds of weird stories. Passers-by had seen the black-robed ghost on the museum grounds, and one had reported that the stone tiger's eyes had actually glowed.

"Personally I think this ghost fellow is playing a walloping big joke on this town," the officer stated, "but we haven't been able to catch him."

"Apparently *we're* involved," said Miss Dana, "and I wish we weren't."

After the police had left, the girls and their aunt continued to discuss the mystery as they unpacked. Finally they went to bed still speculating about it.

At eight o'clock the following morning Cora Appel arrived. She was slightly plump, her blonde hair was stringy, and she walked as if she were about to fall forward. But, as Aunt Harriet often said, Cora had "a heart of gold" and was very loyal to the Danas.

"Hi, everybody!" she cried with an expansive smile. "Am I glad to see you!" She tossed a key onto the kitchen table. "And I won't have to hide that behind the shutter any more!"

Miss Dana and the girls shook hands with Cora, then Louise said, "You didn't carry the key with you?"

"No, ma'm, not me. Why s'pose I was captured on the street by that ghost and he took the key and got in here?"

"I'm afraid that the ghost or someone else saw

you hide the key and came in, anyway," Jean remarked.

When Cora heard about the intruder she flopped into a chair and began to cry. She denied having burned any incense, but sheepishly admitted telling several people when the Danas were expected. "So he found out too, and was here in time to scare you all."

"Now don't take it so hard," Aunt Harriet said soothingly. "Nothing was stolen, and all the intruder did was scare us. Let's forget the whole thing and cook some breakfast."

Cora was too unnerved to be of much help, however, so the others prepared the meal. Jean showed the note for Elise Hilary to Cora and asked when it was delivered.

"I never saw it!" Cora shrieked and burst into tears. "It wasn't on that table when I left here yesterday. The—the ghost must have put it there!" Between sobs, she predicted all sorts of calamities for the Dana family.

"Whee!" said Jean. "It's a good thing I don't believe what you're saying!"

As soon as Louise had finished eating, she telephoned Elise and made a date for the sisters to deliver the note to her at ten o'clock.

"I can't imagine what's in it," Elise said. Louise thought she detected concern in her friend's voice.

At quarter to ten the Dana sisters went to the garage, unlocked it, and got into the car. Louise took the wheel and the girls fastened their seat belts. Then Louise turned the ignition key. As she started to shift into gear, the car suddenly shot forward.

Bang! It hit the rear wall of the garage with a resounding crash!

Louise quickly shut off the motor, as Jean groaned, "Oh, my neck!" She had been thrown backward, then forward, just missing the windscreen. "Feels as if it's broken." Her sister noticed she was pale.

"I'm sorry, Jean. The car wasn't even in gear yet."

"Something's radically wrong with the shift, then. And look at the damage!" Jean responded.

"Never mind that," Louise said. "Let's go into the house." She was sure her sister was about to faint, and helped her from the car.

The crash had brought Aunt Harriet and Cora on the run. Both looked relieved to see the girls on their feet, but Miss Dana insisted that Jean lie down while she called their family doctor.

Cora, seeing the smashed front of the car and the cracked garage wall, cried out, "What did I tell you? The Danas are bewitched! This is just the beginning. Oh dear, oh dear!" She wrung her hands despairingly as they all entered the house.

Louise paid no attention to Cora's dire predictions. "We must have the car towed away and fixed."

"Oh, that reminds me," said Cora. "The other

day the new man from Irving's left a card. They've moved."

Cora found the card in a kitchen drawer. It read:

NEW LOCATION
Irving's Auto Repair Service
Open 24 Hours
519 Main St.
Oak Falls   436-2775

Scribbled at the bottom were the words: *Ask for Emil.*

"We may as well phone him," said Aunt Harriet, and Louise made the call. Emil said he would come within half an hour.

Meanwhile, Dr. Sander arrived. He said Jean's stiff neck was not serious, but prescribed a day of rest in bed. She protested, but to no avail.

"You go over to Elise's, anyway, Louise."

"Okay." Louise phoned, apologizing for being so late and giving the reason. She said she would stop over later in the morning.

As the doctor left, Emil arrived in a tow truck. He was about thirty years of age, short, and boyish looking. He wore triangular-shaped sideburns which, Louise thought, gave him a silly look, and she found his flirtatious smirk annoying. She turned her head away as they walked to the garage.

"Wow!" he exclaimed. "You sure made a wreck out of this bus!"

Louise was startled. "A wreck? Why only the front of the car is damaged."

"That's what you think. A bang like that knocks a whole car out of alignment. Well, nothing to do but to hoist 'er up and take 'er along."

He backed his truck down the driveway to the garage, attached a chain to the rear axle of the Dana car, and pulled it outside, swinging the automobile around in the paved area that fronted the building.

"I sure feel sorry for you," Emil said to Louise, who stood by watching. "Guess you'll have to junk this old crate."

"You mean you can't repair it?" Louise asked, and added spiritedly, "If you can't, leave it alone. I'll call another garage."

"Oh, come now, don't be so touchy over a hunk of metal!" Emil laughed loudly. "You'd do better keeping your sympathy for some man like me. Tell you what. Let me taxi you around while your car's in the shop. How about it?"

Louise could think of nothing worse than such an arrangement. "Thank you," she said icily, "but I'll manage."

"How?"

"I can always walk."

"Choosy, eh? Well, if you change your mind, call the garage. Just ask for me—Emil Gifford at your service."

He got down from the cab, unhooked the chain, then manoeuvred the truck into position so the crane could hoist the front end of the Dana car. With a wave and another expansive smirk at Louise he drove off.

As Louise went back to the house, she thought, "What a creep! I hope I never see him again!"

She reported to Aunt Harriet what Emil had said about the car. "I feel so terrible about it," she said.

Miss Dana hugged her niece affectionately. "It wasn't your fault, dear. Now don't worry any more about it. I'll call the insurance company, and they'll send a man out to look at the car. Perhaps Emil was exaggerating."

Louise felt better and said she would take the bus to the other side of town where the Hilarys lived. She went to tell Jean.

"I feel perfectly okay. Why on earth do I have to stay here?" Jean complained.

"Because Dr. Sander told you to, silly. Anyhow, we have a mystery to solve. Get some rest so we can start our sleuthing."

"At dawn tomorrow," said Jean with a laugh.

Twenty minutes later Louise was ringing the bell of the attractive white cottage on Snowden Drive where Elise and her mother were staying. The estate grounds were on a corner. The museum faced Madison Street and stood about a hundred feet back from the pavement. The building was well screened from both streets by tall trees.

Elise opened the cottage door. "Louise!" she exclaimed, kissing her friend warmly. "How marvellous to see you! When was the last time? Christmas vacation—nearly a year ago."

"That's right—it's been too long," Louise said, gazing at the tall, fair-skinned girl. Elise was twenty-two, had beautiful deep-blue eyes, and thick, gleaming golden hair.

After Louise had expressed her sympathy to Elise at the death of her father, she asked how Mrs. Hilary was.

Elise's voice dropped to a whisper. "Mother isn't well. She's dreadfully nervous and frail. She hasn't recovered from the shock. I'm afraid you can't see her. She asked to be excused."

"I understand and I won't stay long," said Louise. She opened her handbag. "Here is the mysterious note which was left at our house."

"Who in the world could have sent it?" Elise murmured, as she tore open the sealed envelope and took out the printed note.

As she read it, a worried expression came over the young woman's face. "Louise!" she cried in a hoarse whisper. "This is a threat! The note isn't even signed! Listen:

" 'You and your mother must close the museum at once and go on a long trip or your lives will be in danger!' "

CHAPTER III

Good News and Bad

FOR several seconds Louise and Elise just stared at each other. The warning note fluttered to the floor. With trembling fingers, Elise picked it up.

"Louise," she said in a whisper, "what do you think this means?"

"One of two things: either you have an enemy, or someone wants to rob you," Louise replied.

"Enemy? Mother and I have no enemies—at least not that I know of—and I'm *sure* my father didn't—" Elise broke off with a startled gasp. "Oh! Maybe the note has something to do with the prowler in the museum."

"Prowler *in* the museum?" echoed Louise.

"Yes. Our curator, Mr. Pryor, told us some intruder evidently has entered the museum at night." Elise looked baffled. "But if anyone wants to steal from us, why can't he do it while we're home?"

Secretly Louise wondered if the black-robed ghost was the prowler who had entered the museum. Aloud she said, "The only guess I can make now is that the job this person wants to do will take a long time. He probably intends to look for something hidden in the museum."

With a deep sigh, Elise said, "I hope it has nothing to do with my father's exhibits." She added hopefully, "Perhaps whatever this person wants was hidden there long ago."

"Possibly," Louise agreed. "Will you go away?"

"Of course not," Elise answered. "My father brought me up to be brave—and I won't walk out on the museum—his lifework. Mother wouldn't either, even though she's not well."

Suddenly Elise looked towards the ceiling. The girls had heard footsteps on the floor above. "That's Mother," Elise explained, adding, "Louise, she mustn't know anything about this warning. You'll keep my secret, won't you?"

"Of course."

Elise emphasized that her mother was in no condition to have this added worry. The doctor had said she must have complete rest and that any disturbing news should be kept from her.

"Mother isn't able to travel, so we couldn't go on a trip even if we wanted to."

Suddenly Elise's mood changed. Smiling, she said, "Louise, do you know I'm engaged?"

"No. How wonderful! Best wishes! Who is he?"

"His name is Keith Bartlett, and he lives here in town. He's a reporter and feature writer for the *Oak Falls News*."

Louise jumped up from her chair and hugged her friend. "Wait until Jean hears this! She'll be so excited! When are you being married?"

The young woman's lighthearted mood vanished quickly. "Our wedding depends on Keith's job. Right now we're both worried about it. There's a battle going on down at the paper. Keith has offered to buy it from the owner, Mr. Archer."

She told Louise that Keith had inherited some money and planned to use it to purchase the *Oak Falls News*.

"But Mr. Archer is rather a strong-minded old man, and has always taken great pride in what he printed. I guess he doesn't think Keith will keep the paper up to its present standards. Anyway, he's opposed to the idea."

"I love the *News*," said Louise. "Aunt Harriet sends it to Jean and me at school—we wouldn't miss it for anything."

Elise went on to say that Keith Bartlett had promised Mr. Archer he would maintain the paper on the same high level. In line with this, he was trying to have the ghost stories and scares minimized in the *News* so as not to make them appear cheap and sensational.

Louise listened intently as Elise continued, "Mr. Archer received an offer from a big newspaper syndicate. Two men from it are in town and are trying to induce him to sell out. Oddly enough, he listens, which he never would have done before."

"And probably they're offering more money than Keith," Louise guessed.

"Yes. But Keith has investigated the syndicate and is sure that under its direction the *Oak Falls News* would no longer be the fine type of paper this lovely old town should have.

"There's something even worse," Elise went on. "Somebody—and Keith suspects one or both of these newspaper syndicate men—is trying to poison Mr. Archer's mind against Keith. It's an awful mess, but my fiancé is not the type to give up without a fight!"

Louise glanced at the warning note in Elise's hand. "Do you think that the demand for you and your mother to take a trip might have anything to do with this newspaper business and not the museum intruder?"

"I hadn't thought of that," Elise replied. "It might. But it won't do any good. I'm not leaving Keith."

In turn she asked Louise what explanation she had for the note being left at the Dana house.

"The only reason I can think of," said Louise, "is that the person who wrote it probably overheard either Cora Appel or someone else say that Jean and I like to solve mysteries and he hopes to deter us from interfering in this one."

"Whoever this strange person is, he doesn't know you two!" said Elise, smiling.

As she was speaking, the front doorbell rang. Elise answered and Louise heard her say, "Keith! Hi! . . . Has something gone wrong?"

"Nothing but another session with Mr. Archer. He's not only stubborn, but now acting strangely!"

Elise came into the living room, followed by Keith. He was tall, with an athletic build and dark, slightly wavy hair. His brown eyes, Louise guessed, were usually happy and twinkling. Now, she thought, they seemed troubled.

"Elise has often told me about you and your sister," he said, after the introductions were made. "You've been having a gay time on your Western trip."

"Yes, we have," said Louise, "and plenty of excitement, too."

Elise laughed. "The girls just arrived home last night and more excitement started for them right in Oak Falls."

She held up the warning note for her fiancé to read. "This was left mysteriously at the Danas' house," she told him, and handed over the note.

Keith read the note and his expression became grim. "I don't like this," he said. "Any idea who might have sent it, Elise?"

"Not the slightest, and Louise hasn't either."

"Unless," said Louise, "it was the black-robed ghost."

"What!" Keith exclaimed.

Louise told how Cora Appel had been startled by the ghost near the kitchen door of their home. "Cora hid the key, and we have a hunch the ghost found it and unlocked the door."

"That could be," Keith agreed. "I'm sorry you Danas are involved. So far, this strange character hasn't done anything but scare people, but I think that if he doesn't accomplish his purpose, he may become more dangerous and *really* harm someone."

Louise now revealed her theory that the museum intruder might be the ghost. Keith conceded this was likely, since the black-robed figure had been seen on the estate grounds at night.

Elise shivered. "And, of course, people have seen other odd things around town." She turned to her fiancé. "Mother mustn't hear a word about this warning note."

"You're right." Keith promised to keep it a secret. "In fact," he added, "no one outside of the few who already know about the note should hear of it except the police."

Louise drew a long breath. "I'll speak to Cora as soon as I get home, but there's no telling how many people she may have told already. She's a terrific gossip."

Suddenly Elise turned to Louise. "Would you Danas try solving this mystery of the black-robed ghost? Not only for Mother's sake and Keith's and mine—but for everyone else in town."

Louise smiled, and now confided to the engaged couple that she and her sister had already resolved to undertake the challenge.

Elise brightened immediately. "Oh, wonderful! I just know you'll have success."

Keith also looked encouraged. "Great!" he said. "Let us know if we can be of any help."

"I will." Louise laughed. "If you find any clues, be sure to get in touch with us."

The young detective then explained that she was a bit anxious about Jean, and thought she should go home to see her. Back at the Dana house, she found her sister sitting up in bed, talking to Aunt Harriet, and demanding a large luncheon.

"That's encouraging to hear," said Miss Dana. "Suppose the three of us eat right here."

"Wonderful idea!" said Jean.

A few minutes later Louise and Cora carried the trays upstairs.

"*Um!*" cried Jean. "Chicken salad, hot rolls, sliced tomatoes, and chocolate ice cream with angel cake—*hm*—not bad for a starter," she added with a grin.

While the Danas were eating, Louise told about her visit to the Hilary home. "And guess what! Elise is engaged! To an absolute dreamboat! His name is Keith Bartlett!"

Then Louise sobered and told about the trouble at the newspaper, the warning note, and the museum intruder.

Aunt Harriet looked greatly disturbed and Jean frowned, saying, "This mystery is turning out to be a double-header!" She gave an impatient sigh. "I want to get out of bed and start sleuthing around the Hilary estate right now!"

"Not until tomorrow," Aunt Harriet said firmly.

"Before we go downtown or to the museum or anywhere else," Louise spoke up, "I think we should look for clues in our own house. After all, the person we're trying to find *was* here!"

Louise's next sentence was lost in a sudden blood-curdling scream from the first floor.

"Oh, what happened?" cried Miss Dana.

Louise dashed from the room, followed by her aunt. The two rushed pell-mell down the stairs.

CHAPTER IV

Midnight Crash

CORA APPEL was stumbling from the Dana living room. There was terror in her eyes.

"What happened?" Louise asked her quickly.

The maid did not answer. Staring straight ahead, almost as if she were sightless, the frightened woman made a beeline for the kitchen. Louise and Aunt Harriet followed. At once Cora collapsed onto a chair and folded her head in her arms. She began to weep hysterically.

"What *is* it?" Aunt Harriet prodded. "We can't do anything until you explain."

Cora began to mumble incoherently. She twisted nervously in her seat and the only words the Danas could make out were ". . . that ghost in black! . . . Oh, he's put a spell on us! . . . He'll kill all of us!"

Unable to draw anything further from Cora, both Louise and her aunt hurried back to the living room. They saw that the large couch had been pulled away from the wall. On the floor behind it lay a black turban and a small green snake!

"These must have been what frightened Cora," said Louise.

"But where—where did they come from?" Aunt Harriet gasped. As Louise leaned over to pick up the snake, Miss Dana cried out, "Don't touch that!"

Louise laughed. "Aunt Harriet, this isn't a real snake."

Miss Dana looked a little sheepish, though relieved. "Even so," she said, "it may have poison in it or something else dangerous."

Her niece admitted that this was possible. "Cora might be right in thinking that the black-robed ghost left both objects." Louise picked up the turban, which was a cheap machine-made version of the lovely headgear worn in India.

India again!

Aunt Harriet went directly to the telephone and called police headquarters. Sergeant Renley, who had been assigned to the case, and was on overtime duty, came on the phone.

"I'll be right over," he said.

Meanwhile, Louise had gone into the kitchen and had finally managed to get a lucid explanation from Cora about her discovery. The maid said that she had pulled out the couch, intending to mop the floor behind it. Seeing the turban had not disturbed her, for she had concluded that one of the Danas accidentally might have dropped it there.

"But when I picked it up and that horrible snake fell out—my heart did a flip-flop! I don't care if the snake isn't real, it *looks* real! Oh, what are we going to do? Lately, every time I've come to this house something awful's happened!"

Miss Dana, who had been listening from the doorway, said kindly, "Cora, how would you like to go home for the rest of the day? The police are coming to see about the turban and the snake, and I know they'll want to talk to you, but after that you may leave."

"Oh, thank you, ma'am," Cora said gratefully. "I don't mean to be a scaredy-cat, Miss Dana, but you've got to admit what's been goin' on here just ain't right."

"It is unusual," Aunt Harriet agreed. "But," she added, with an effort at reassurance, "I'm sure the girls will solve the mystery soon."

Louise returned to the living room for the turban and the snake, which she picked up in a paper towel. She carried them upstairs to show Jean. The sisters could find no clues to indicate their owner's identity. But both girls felt sure that the wearer had removed the black turban containing the snake while arranging the eerie display in the window the night before.

"He probably laid it on the back of the couch," Jean reasoned, "and it fell to the floor."

"Yes," Louise agreed. "And, in his haste to leave the note for Elise and look around our house for whatever he's interested in, he forgot to retrieve his property."

Jean suddenly giggled. "Weird getups in this mystery! A ghost in black—and someone wearing a snake in his turban!"

By now, Sergeant Renley and another policeman had arrived. They took out fingerprinting equipment and lifted several samples of prints from the couch and a small table next to it. Sergeant Renley dropped the turban and the snake into a bag he carried, questioned Cora and the Danas, then left. Almost immediately, the maid put on her coat and hat and said good-bye.

Jean laughed upon learning her aunt had suggested that Cora go home. "Maybe this is the last we'll see of dear old Applecore at our house. She sure has had a lot of scares lately. And she's one up on us—we haven't yet seen the ghost with the black robe."

"Let's hope we do soon," Louise said eagerly. "It might give us a start to solving this mystery."

"Well, tomorrow we go to the museum," said Jean. "I feel fine—really I do. I'd set off right now if that fussy old doctor would let me."

The three Danas had a quiet supper in Jean's bedroom and all of them retired early. Later they were awakened suddenly from sound sleep by a terrific crash. The two sisters and their aunt hurriedly got out of bed and met in the hall.

"Something fell against the house!" Jean exclaimed.

She and the others quickly put on robes and slippers, then ran from room to room to see if any of the walls had been damaged. They were not.

"Maybe it was a tree," Aunt Harriet suggested.

They looked from the windows but saw no fallen tree.

"I'm going outside," Jean declared.

She grabbed a flashlight from the drawer in the hall table and dashed out the front door. Louise followed, but Miss Dana decided to stand guard inside, in case the noise had been a ruse to lure them all out of the house.

The two girls ran to the side of the house nearest the driveway. Suddenly both stopped. A very tall ladder, reaching to an attic window, stood against the house. No one was on it.

"Maybe someone got in through the attic window!" Jean ventured.

"I'll stay here and see if anyone comes out," Louise offered. "Why don't you and Aunt Harriet see if there's an intruder in the house?"

"Okay."

Jean hurried back to the front hall where Miss Dana still waited. Upon hearing her niece's suspicion, she started up the stairway with Jean. They investigated the second-floor rooms, but searching for an intruder in the attic was more than Miss Dana cared to risk.

"I'll telephone the police again," she said.

This time two different officers came. They could find no one hiding in the attic, but said that the window up there was unlocked. "I fastened it," said one of them, who identified himself as Officer Brownell.

The policemen made a thorough search of the grounds and garage, but detected no signs of an intruder or any distinguishable footprints.

"Does this ladder belong to you?" Officer Gibbs asked.

"Yes," Louise replied. "It's an extension ladder we store in our garage."

"Well," Officer Gibbs responded, "I'd say definitely someone intended to enter your house by the attic window. Your ladder was so heavy, that when he leaned it against the building, he lost his grasp and the ladder fell against the house, causing the loud noise which awakened you. He must have run away without climbing it.

"By the way," the policeman continued, "Sergeant Renley says that all the fingerprints were left by the same person, but aren't on record."

Officer Gibbs assured the Danas that he would stay near the house during the rest of the night in case the intruder should return. But morning came without incident and the ladder was removed by

Officer Gibbs and another officer who came in a car to pick him up.

Cora arrived a little later, looking pale and shaky. The Danas decided to spare the young woman's feelings and did not tell her about the episode of the previous night. While the two sisters and their aunt were eating breakfast in the dining room, Cora answered a knock at the back door. The caller was Emil Gifford from Irving's Auto Repair Service.

"Hi! Fancy seein' you again!" the breezy young man said. "You're Cora Appel from across town, aren't you?"

Cora looked questioningly at Emil Gifford. "How'd you know my name?" she asked. "I didn't tell you when you were here before."

"Why, you're famous in town—don't you work for the Dana Detective Service?" He grinned mockingly.

"I work for the Dana family," said Cora, trying to appear dignified. "I suppose you came about the car?"

"Yep. I wanna talk to Louise."

"She's busy," said Cora. "And I don't like your manners."

"You don't, eh?" Emil laughed. "Well, see if I care what you like. Go get Louise."

He opened the door wider and entered the kitchen. Cora turned and walked into the dining room.

"That man from the repair place is here. He wants to see you, Miss Louise."

Slightly amused at Cora's unusual formality, Louise left the table and went to see Emil. As she entered the kitchen, he smiled broadly.

"Hello, gorgeous!" he said, winking. "Wish I had better news for you. The insurance adjuster was down to our place. They sure don't wanna give you much money. What they'll pay won't begin to cover the expense of fixing your car."

"What!" Louise exclaimed. "I didn't do *that* much damage!"

"Oh, no?" Emil Gifford laughed raucously. "Women don't know beans about automobiles. I could fill a book tellin' you everything that's wrong. My advice to you is to scrap the old buggy."

Louise gasped. She thought, with a sinking sensation, that she and she alone was responsible for what had happened. Furthermore, the Danas had spent so much on their trip to the West that they could not possibly afford a new car at this time.

"I'm sorry, awful sorry," said Emil. "Now maybe you'll take up my offer. I told you it wouldn't cost you a nickel for me to taxi you around. How about it? Where do you wanna go this mornin'?"

Louise simply stared at the mechanic. "Nowhere, thank you," she replied curtly.

Emil moved closer. "If not today, how about you and me goin' to a movie some night?"

Emil Gifford was obnoxious, Louise thought. The sooner she could get rid of him the better!

"Please don't ask me again to go anywhere with you," she said firmly. "You're very kind to offer, but I have other plans."

Emil apparently was not offended, and he merely shrugged. As he opened the back door, the mechanic said, "Like I told you before, if you change your mind, let me know."

After he had gone, Cora remarked, "You wouldn't be datin' a man like that, would you?"

Louise laughed. "You heard what I told him."

Miss Dana and Jean, who had remained in the dining room, were more amused than worried over the attention Louise was receiving. When she returned to the table, the conversation centred around the problem of the car.

"Let me think the whole thing out," said Aunt Harriet. "You girls go on to the museum and start your sleuthing."

Jean and Louise got their coats, then walked to the corner to catch the bus which ran past the Hilary estate. They got off near the museum and hurried up the long, winding path which was bordered by oak and maple trees. Approaching the building, the sisters stopped and gazed in awe.

"The stone tiger—it's beautiful!" Louise exclaimed. "A real work of art!"

CHAPTER V

Mongoose Attack

As Louise and Jean gazed at the stone tiger, they decided it was one of the most beautiful pieces of sculpture they had ever seen. The beast was life-size, fashioned from snow-white, black-grained marble. It stood erect with the head slightly tilted as if the tiger were listening for sounds of an approaching enemy.

"He's gorgeous!" Jean exclaimed. "And he must weigh a ton!"

Louise nodded as her eyes travelled downward to the attractive ebony pedestal upon which the animal was mounted.

"That tiger is perfect at the entrance to this handsome museum," she remarked.

"It certainly is," Jean agreed. "What a shame that Mr. Hilary never saw the maharajah's gift to him! Louise, I'm pretty sure of one thing about this mystery connected with the museum: Nobody plans to steal the stone tiger—he's much too heavy."

"Unless, of course," said Louise, "people had a long time in which to hoist him onto a truck. Keith Bartlett said that police patrols go past here about every half-hour, so there wouldn't be much chance for a thief to make off with the tiger."

"Which means," said Jean, "that the cause of the mystery *must* be inside the museum."

"Let's go in and see if the curator can shed any light on it," Louise urged.

The sisters mounted the wide steps onto the portico of the stately old Georgian mansion. Louise rang the bell. After a long wait the door was opened by a rather short man about fifty years old. He was slightly overweight but rugged looking, with reddish crew-cut hair.

He smiled and held the door wide. "Won't you come in?"

"Thank you." Louise paid the admission fee.

"I'm the curator here. My name's Patrick Pryor. Will you please register?"

Mr. Pryor led the Danas into the spacious centre hall with oak-panelled walls. On a table, next to a telephone, lay a guest book and a pen. The girls noticed that Mr. Pryor walked with a decided limp. As the sisters signed the book, the curator said:

"I'm not busy. I'll be glad to show you around."

"Fine. Thank you." Louise smiled.

Mr. Pryor looked at the girls quizzically and asked, "Do you, by any chance, belong to the Dana family the Hilarys know?"

"Yes," Louise answered. "Our families have been friends for years."

"Then you're the girls who can solve mysteries," Mr. Pryor said, beaming. "I certainly wish you'd solve the mystery of this museum!"

Jean laughed. "That's one reason we're here," she explained. "We'd like to start right now, and would appreciate any help you can give us."

Mr. Pryor sighed. "I wish I could, but Elise and I haven't figured out anything."

He led the way into a small parlour to the right of the hall. Each wall contained a series of shelves on which stood the smaller animals that Mr. Hilary had shot or trapped in India. Among them were exquisitely coloured parrots, several mongooses, and wild dogs.

"They look so lifelike, they're scary," Jean remarked.

Mr. Pryor laughed. "I sometimes wish they were! They might be able to nab the person who sneaked in here secretly at night over a week ago."

"Was anything taken?" Louise asked the curator quickly.

"No. I figure the sneak didn't find what he was looking for. But glass display cases were forced open."

"Do you think," Jean spoke up, "that the intruder was the black-robed ghost who has been scaring people in town?"

"I suppose he could've been," Mr. Pryor said.

He next led the way across the hall to a very large room on the far side. As the sisters entered it, they gasped in astonishment. In the centre of the floor stood several huge display cases. One contained a fine specimen of a water buffalo. Another held a rhinoceros just rising out of lucid water. In a third stood a half-grown elephant with its trunk raised into the air.

With a note of pride in his voice, Mr. Pryor said, "I helped collect all these animals. I used to trek through the jungles with Mr. Hilary. Unfortunately, a hunter's stray bullet got me in the knee. The injury caused the end of my safari days."

"That's too bad," said Louise. "You certainly did your part in providing this fine collection of jungle animals."

The curator led the way down one side of the room and up the other. In their tour the girls passed a wolf, a striped hyena, and several yellow tigers.

"Mr. Hilary was especially fond of tigers," said Mr. Pryor. "Contrary to what most people think, these animals are great cowards. There are many old legends about cunning men getting the better of them. One of the sports of ancient Indian princes was to pit tigers against bulls and buffaloes, which the cats feared. They knew the tiger would make every effort to keep out of his antagonist's way, and to the onlookers, this was great sport."

"Are there actually any white tigers?" Jean asked. "We think the statue in front of the museum is marvellous."

Mr. Pryor said that one area of India, the wide forests of Rewa, near the cities of Allahabad and Mirzapur, is the breeding ground for white tigers.

"They are the rarest of all the cat family," he explained. "Their coats are eggshell white and their eyes ice blue. With their black stripes, these beasts are striking, indeed."

The curator went on to say that to him it seemed strange that lions, griffons, monkeys, and elephants are often depicted in Indian art but rarely tigers.

"This may be because this animal is considered the symbol of cowardice," said Mr. Pryor. "There's one legend I particularly like. It's about a mouse deer being chased by a tiger. As he was running off, the mouse deer stopped to eat berries and thus made his mouth very red. Finally, knowing he could not outdistance the tiger because he was tiring rapidly, the mouse deer sat down by a well.

"As the tiger overtook him and crouched to attack, the mouse deer said, 'Watch out! I have killed many tigers!' The beast confronting him gazed at the mouse deer's mouth and thought the redness was blood. However, he wavered, so the mouse deer said, 'If you don't believe me, look into the well.'

"When the tiger gazed down into the water, he saw a reflection of himself, but thought it was the head of a tiger the mouse deer had killed. Like a coward he ran away as fast as he could."

Louise and Jean laughed, and Louise said, "I love some of those old legends. They certainly *do* illustrate character traits in people and animals—such as shrewdness, or timidity."

As the girls walked on, they looked from shelf to shelf, filled with many other wild animals. There were dholes—a ferocious kind of wild dog—and several more specimens of mongoose.

Suddenly Jean cried out, "Look out, Louise!"

At that moment an animal from one of the shelves above Louise's head plummeted directly towards her. Just in the nick of time Jean pulled her sister to safety.

A stuffed mongoose on its heavy pedestal landed at Louise's feet.

"I'm sorry!" said Mr. Pryor. "I thought all the animals were secure."

"This one didn't move by itself!" Jean declared. "I saw a human hand throw that mongoose down here!"

She dashed from the room and into the hall. Jean looked up the stairway, half expecting to see someone there—whoever she had seen reaching through the panelled wall. But no one was in sight.

By this time Louise and Mr. Pryor had reached her side. "Someone else is in this building!" Jean insisted.

The Danas, noting that the landing on the stairway was in line with the display-room shelf from which the mongoose had been thrown, hurried up the steps and began to examine the panels.

"One of these may be movable and reveal a closet or secret stairway," Jean declared.

Excitedly the two girls and Mr. Pryor tapped, pushed, and pulled at the various panels on the landing. None would move.

"Perhaps there's some secret device or a combination of two panels," Louise suggested.

First the sisters tried pushing against two panels at a time. This did not work. Next, they began pressing alternate sections at the same time. Suddenly Jean found the combination!

CHAPTER VI

Curator's Dilemma

MR. PRYOR moved closer to Louise and Jean, curious to see what lay beyond the opening panel. The section between the two which Jean had been pressing, now slid back completely behind the other panel. The trio peered in. Beyond was a tall, narrow space between the wall of the stairway and that of the museum's large display room.

"Nobody here!" said the curator in disappointment.

"The person must have run to the second floor," Louise suggested. "Let's go and find out."

It was decided that one of the three searchers should remain behind to guard the lower part of the house, so Louise offered to stay on the main floor. Mr. Pryor and Jean hurried on upstairs. They searched every room, every closet, and looked under the furniture. There was no one around, so the two started up the wide stairway to the third storey. Here again they had no luck.

"I just can't understand it," said Mr. Pryor, shaking his head and frowning.

As he and Jean came back down, she remarked, "The person who heaved that mongoose did a ghostlike disappearing act."

She reported their failure to find anyone to Louise, who stood waiting on the landing of the stairway.

"There may be more secret openings—even entrances to this building," Louise remarked. "While you both were gone, I tried to figure out how the mysterious person got his hand through this back wall to throw the mongoose."

Louise admitted she had not yet discovered the secret. "I didn't dare step on the floor in there for fear it actually might be a trap door, but if you two will hold onto me, I can get close enough to work on the wall."

The floor of the concealed space was found to be solid, and after further investigation, Louise discovered a movable small square of wood in the wall. She took out the piece and peered through at the shelf on the other side.

"This is exactly where the mongoose stood!" Louise exclaimed.

She stepped back onto the landing and slid the panelled sections into place. Then the three mystified searchers returned to the first floor.

"That small opening into the big room," said Mr. Pryor, "probably was an old-time peephole. In some of the elegant old homes of a century or more ago, the owners often had such places built in. From these vantage points they could watch callers they did not entirely trust—or servants whom they suspected might not be strictly honest."

"Do you think the Hilarys know about this peephole?" Louise asked the curator.

"No," Mr. Pryor replied. "I'm sure they would have mentioned it to me if they did."

"Then the person who used the hidden room a short while ago must be familiar with the architecture of this house," Jean concluded.

The others agreed, but were still puzzled as to how the intruder had entered and left the mansion.

"We've found nothing," said Louise, "to explain the attempt to knock me out."

Jean remarked that if the intruder was the ghost in the black robe, at least she knew what one of his hands looked like. She grinned. "That's not much of an identification, is it?"

"Are you sure every door and window in the museum is tightly locked?" Louise quizzed the curator.

"Positive."

"Is there a cellar with an entrance that could be broken into?" Jean questioned him.

Mr. Pryor said that the only entrance to the

basement was through the kitchen. The cellar windows, he added, were small and high, with bars, so no one could have entered the house that way.

"I'll feel better if you girls see this for yourselves," Mr. Pryor told them. "Please follow me."

Louise and Jean assured the man they did not doubt him, but he insisted that they come along. The group entered the kitchen. The door to the cellar was locked, as was the rear entrance. Upon checking the windows, the Danas saw that the lock on each was securely fastened.

Finally they were back in the main hall. Mr. Pryor made no move to investigate the front door, so Jean walked forward and opened it. She turned the knob from the outside.

"Why, this door's unlocked!" she exclaimed.

Mr. Pryor dashed over and tried it himself. Suddenly he became very pale and cried out excitedly, "This is how the intruder got in here today! Some visitor to this place must have unlatched the door. I admit I never tried the knob from the outside because the door locks automatically. Oh, how stupid of me!"

Louise spoke up, "You haven't had many visitors lately, I understand. I should think that might make it easier for you to find out who did this."

Mr. Pryor locked the door and the three walked over to the guest book. Louise's and Jean's names were at the top of a page. Now Mr. Pryor turned back to the preceding one. He ran his finger up the page. One of the names caught the Danas' eyes.

" 'Mrs. Emil Gifford,' " Louise read. "Is she the wife of the mechanic at Irving's Auto Repair Service?"

"I really don't know," the curator replied. "She came here with her friend—Mrs. Crocker—the name just below," he added, pointing. "I recall a short man came to the door with them."

To herself Louise was saying, "If this *is* the wife of that pest, then he had some nerve trying to date me!"

Jean apparently was thinking the same thing, for she gave her sister a knowing look. Moreover, both girls noted that the women and all the succeeding callers had been to the museum three days ago. No one had come since.

When Mr. Pryor also realized this, he exclaimed, "That door has been unlocked for at least three days! My carelessness may cause the Hilarys even more trouble." The curator paced back and forth, obviously chagrined at himself. "Maybe I'd better resign."

Louise looked at the man sympathetically. "We all make mistakes," she said kindly. "I'm sure you wouldn't really want to leave here. Do you remember when you last checked the front door?"

The curator thought for nearly a minute, then said, "A week ago."

Jean brightened. "Then there's no proof the in-

truder came by the front door. Wasn't it over
a week ago that your display cases were broken
into?"

"That's right. And the police found no signs of
forced entry."

The curator looked relieved for a few seconds,
then his face clouded. "This means the intruder
unlatches the door or knows a secret way of getting into the building. I must ask the police to come
past here and check even more often than they
have been doing."

Louise suggested that they hunt for tangible
clues to the intruder.

"Sensible idea," said Mr. Pryor. "I'd like to see
how you girl detectives operate."

He watched with great interest as he followed
the two young sleuths. They examined the walls
and floor around the peephole, stairway, and hall,
and finally returned to the large display room.

Louise immediately picked up the mongoose
which had been hurled at her. She scrutinized its
fur, then suddenly cried out, "Here's something in
its mouth!"

She inserted a finger into the opening between
the teeth and pulled out a large ring.

Mr. Pryor stared at the plain gold band, with a
red stone in a crownlike setting. "It's probably a
man's ring," he observed, "and definitely of Indian
origin!"

"Indian?" Jean repeated. "This could be a marvellous clue. The ring must have slipped off the man's finger just before he threw the mongoose. Now we should hunt up all the people in town who have ever lived in India or visited there."

"That sounds like quite a job," Mr. Pryor remarked. "You'd better leave it to the police."

"It would be hard, all right," Louise agreed. "Jean, why don't we try Elise first? She may possibly recognize this ring!"

CHAPTER VII

Eerie Music

ELISE HILARY was surprised and delighted to see the Dana girls.

"I was going to get in touch with you," she said. "Something has happened—I want to tell you about it."

The three friends sat down in the cottage living room. "First," said Louise, "we'd like to tell you something interesting."

"I'd like to hear it," Elise replied eagerly.

From her handbag Louise took the ring which had been found in the mouth of the mongoose. She handed it to Elise. "Have you ever seen this before?" Louise asked her.

"It does look vaguely familiar. Where did you get the ring?"

As Louise and Jean related the story, Elise's eyes grew wide. Finally she burst out, "How dreadful! Louise, I'm certainly glad you weren't hurt. I had no idea when I asked you girls to help solve the mystery that anything this dangerous would happen."

Jean laughed. "When you're a detective, you expect to run into trouble once in a while!"

"That's all right for a man who makes a business of being a detective," Elise said. "But you're my friends and I wouldn't want anything to happen to you on my account."

The sisters assured Elise that they would be careful. Louise added, "It's too late to stop us now, anyway. We're in this mystery pretty deep. Jean and I are determined to find out who's responsible for the queer things that have been going on in town and at the museum."

Elise turned the gold ring over and over in her hand, looking inside for some identifying mark. She could find nothing.

"Is the ring valuable?" Jean asked Elise.

"Not particularly."

"Then the person who lost it won't bother to come back to look for it," Louise guessed. "That means the police wouldn't bother to set a trap for the fellow."

Elise continued to study the ring. "I believe I know *why* this seems familiar," she said. "Such rings are common in India and I saw many of them while I was there. But the whole thing is terribly disturbing."

"I'll turn it over to the police," Louise decided. Then, realizing that Elise was becoming upset, she quickly changed the subject. "You said you had something to tell us," she said.

"That's right."

Elise told the Danas that there had been a disagreeable scene at the newspaper office. "Those men, Mr. Homer and Mr. Semple, practically threatened Mr. Archer. They insisted upon buying the newspaper, and when Mr. Archer said he had not fully made up his mind, the men began saying perfectly dreadful things about Keith."

Elise went on, her eyes filling with tears. "They said he was just a young nobody and would ruin the paper."

"How mean!" Jean cried in sympathy. "Mr. Archer didn't pay any attention to their remarks, did he?"

"That old man is unpredictable. All he did was listen—he didn't stand up for Keith at all, but my fiancé came to his own defence. He told those two men a few things. Afterwards, Keith was sure Mr. Archer would discharge him, but instead he ordered the syndicate men to leave!"

The Danas tried to assure Elise that this was a good sign, but she only sighed. "There's more to the story," she explained. "Mr. Homer and Mr. Semple are making up stories about the Hilary family. When Keith told me what they were I nearly died. They implied that my father wasn't honest and anybody who married into this family would be sorry."

Louise's face showed her disgust. "Mr. Homer and Mr. Semple sound like a couple of trouble-makers," she declared. "*I* wouldn't pay any attention to them, and I'm sure Mr. Archer didn't believe what they said."

"Then why didn't he tell them so?" Elise cried out. "He won't even listen to Keith's offer and promises to keep the paper as it is now. Louise and Jean, would you do me a favour—and talk to Mr. Archer?"

"Us?" Jean stared in surprise. "What do you think *we* could do?"

Elise smiled. "I've seen you perform other miracles," she said coaxingly.

The sisters finally consented to call on the newspaper owner. In a few minutes they left Elise and hurried to their own home.

"I think it will make a better impression on Mr. Archer if Aunt Harriet goes with us," Louise said thoughtfully.

When they asked Miss Dana if she would accompany them to the *Oak Falls News* office to talk with Mr. Archer, a strange expression came over their aunt's face. She looked off into space and slowly a deep blush spread over her face. The girls waited, puzzled by Aunt Harriet's reaction.

"Louise and Jean," she said at last, "there was a time when Mr. Archer and I used to go out together, but even in those days he was pretty dictatorial. After a while I refused to have any more dates with him."

The sisters were amazed to hear this. They knew that Aunt Harriet had been a very pretty and popular young woman and had heard the names of several men whom she had dated, but Mr. Archer had not been one of them.

Louise smiled affectionately at her aunt. "Does this mean you'd rather not call on him?"

Miss Dana's eyes twinkled. "I won't go so far as to say that I wouldn't," she replied. "But it *will* seem kind of funny."

She consented to telephoning the *News* office and making an appointment for ten o'clock Saturday morning.

"Oh, I forgot to tell you!" Aunt Harriet exclaimed to her nieces. "Jane Humphrey called you a little earlier. She'd like to come over this afternoon."

"Wonderful!" exclaimed Jean. "Why don't we invite the whole group here, Louise? We haven't seen our Oak Falls friends in ages."

Louise was enthusiastic about the idea, so the sisters took turns calling their friends. They found that six girls could come.

"What shall we have for a snack?" Louise asked.

"How about tiny open-face melted-cheese sandwiches?" Aunt Harriet suggested.

"Perfect!" said Louise. "And we can serve cocoa with them."

Miss Dana told the girls she had a fruitcake which she would donate to the party for dessert. "I made it just before we went on our trip. By now it is well aged."

"I know it'll be yummy." Jean smiled.

From the moment Cora Appel heard that guests were expected, she became more and more nervous. She gave the living room a second dusting, and while doing it, knocked down a vase and stumbled over a hassock.

"It's just that I ain't used to company lately," she said apologetically. "But I'll be all right. You just take care o' your friends and I'll do the cookin'."

Louise and Jean secretly were not sure this would be a safe arrangement, but after their visitors arrived and Aunt Harriet had left to do some shopping, they forgot about Cora. Within a few minutes everybody was talking at once. The Danas' friends wanted to hear about their marvellous trip. Louise and Jean in turn hoped to catch up on local teen-age news.

"You've come back to a scary old town," said Jane Humphrey. "Oh, I wish something could be done! You Danas ought to solve the mystery."

Jean laughed. "We're trying to, but haven't had any luck yet."

"Everybody is afraid to be out on the street after dark," Jane went on, "and our annual Cloverleaf Girls Club dance is Saturday."

"You shouldn't let that ghost scare you," said Louise. "He's probably no worse than a Halloween prankster. He hasn't hurt anybody yet."

Another visitor, Mimi Trost, asked, "Louise and Jean, you'll come to the dance?"

Louise smiled. "We'd love to. Maybe we can scare up dates in time." She was thinking of Ken Scott and Chris Barton, whom the sisters dated when at Starhurst School.

The conversation suddenly was interrupted by an outcry from the kitchen. Louise and Jean rushed off to find out what had happened. Cora stood near the stove. The oven door was open and every little melted-cheese sandwich was burned to a crisp!

"Oh, it's terrible! Terrible!" Cora wailed. "Why did I ever say I'd cook these things? Everything is ruined. What we goin' to do?"

"Make some more," said Louise.

Cora meekly got out the bread and began cutting it into small pieces. Jean quickly fixed slices of cheese and arranged them on the bread. Louise started to prepare the cocoa.

"Cora, would you get out the fruitcake and slice it?" she asked.

In a short time the refreshments were ready. Louise and Jean decided that Cora had better not carry the food into the living room, so they did it themselves. Their friends enjoyed the snack, and laughed over the sisters' description of the burned sandwiches.

Jane whispered to the Danas, "What would this house do without Cora? You always have a good story to tell us about her."

"Poor Applecore!" said Jean. "But she's the best-hearted person in the world."

The flustered maid did not recover from her embarrassment and dismay. While helping to prepare supper, she dropped one dish and two saucepans. Afterwards, Cora sheepishly confessed that she was afraid to go out on the street alone to return to her home.

"Been on my mind all day," she added. "Guess that's why I've done everything wrong."

"Would you like to stay here tonight?" Aunt Harriet asked her.

"Oh, no! Too many funny things have happened in this house at night," Cora declared. "But I was thinkin', couldn't some o' you walk home with me?"

Louise and Jean said they would be glad to.

"And I'll go along," Miss Dana stated. "I'm sure there'll be safety in numbers."

After the Danas had left Cora at her house, they decided to walk past the Hilary Museum. They stood looking at the old mansion from the pavement. Except for the light in the entrance hall, the building was in darkness.

"Let's walk up to the museum," Jean suggested.

"It may be a rash thing to do," Aunt Harriet pointed out, but she followed the girls along the front walk.

Just as they reached the museum, Louise grabbed her sister's arm. "Listen!" she whispered.

Seemingly from inside the museum came the weird tones of haunting flute music.

"How strange!" said Aunt Harriet in a low voice, and Jean added, "It's positively spooky."

Louise said, "That flute music sounds just like the type snake charmers play!"

CHAPTER VIII

Vanishing Fugitive

CHILLS of excitement ran up and down the Danas' spines as the queer music continued.

A moment later Aunt Harriet said firmly, "This should be reported to the police at once. Shall we go over to the Hilary cottage and make the call?"

Her nieces agreed and the three started off.

Suddenly Louise cried, "Wait!" A patrol car had stopped in front of the museum grounds, and two policemen alighted. The Danas hurried to meet Officers Brownell and Gibbs and quickly explained about the flute music, which by now had ceased.

As Officer Brownell started towards the back of the mansion, the other policeman asked, "Are you sure the music came from inside the building?"

"We couldn't say positively," Aunt Harriet replied. "But it certainly sounded like it."

Officer Gibbs went up to try the main door and found it locked. Then he started across the front of the house, beaming his flashlight into each window. Presently he disappeared around the side.

As the Danas stood waiting for a report, Jean suddenly exclaimed, "Look! I see a man running away!"

The shadowy figure was racing pell-mell across the grounds towards the Hilary cottage. He had come from the side of the museum which the officers apparently had not yet checked.

"Let's follow him!" Louise urged, and she and Jean raced after the figure.

Aunt Harriet, meanwhile, dashed to the rear of the building to alert the policemen.

By this time the girls had lost sight of the fleeing man, and though they separated and looked behind trees and the low hedge, they did not see the fugitive. Presently, not far from the Hilary cottage, they were joined by the two officers. Aunt Harriet, moving at a slower pace, finally caught up to them. Using flashlights, the two officers made an exhaustive survey of the grounds and both Madison Street and Snowden Drive, but did not find anyone.

The group walked back and examined the side of the museum from which the intruder had come. Every window was locked and none of them broken.

"I guess your flute player wasn't inside after all," Officer Brownell concluded.

The Danas did not disagree but thought there

was a good possibility he had been. The girls still felt strongly that the intruder had a key or knew some secret entrance to the old house. Meanwhile, Officer Gibbs had gone to the patrol car to notify headquarters. The captain in turn telephoned Mr. Pryor, who drove over at once.

"The Danas may have foiled an attempted robbery," Officer Gibbs told him. "However, the person they saw running away may have stolen something. Will you please check and see if anything is missing from the museum?"

After a thorough search was made, Mr. Pryor reported that he had found nothing missing.

"You say someone was playing the flute?" he asked the girls.

"Yes, but not American style," Louise replied. "It sounded like the weird music played by snake charmers."

Mr. Pryor turned towards the police. "I am inclined to think that the mystery of Oak Falls and the Hilary Museum are somehow connected with India."

Louise then asked the officers if they knew whether anyone from that country was staying in Oak Falls. "No one suspicious," Officer Gibbs replied. "But we'll keep checking that angle."

The museum was locked once more and everyone prepared to leave. The police said they would assign a guard to the grounds during the night.

The Danas were about to start homewards when

Louise said, "It isn't late. Why don't we stop to see Elise? I'd like to tell her about our date with Mr. Archer and what happened tonight."

"Good idea," Jean replied, and Aunt Harriet agreed.

When they arrived at the Hilary cottage, Elise opened the door. She smiled, but the girls thought she looked particularly worried. Louise told her what had just taken place at the museum, but assured Elise that the police were putting on a special guard for the night.

Elise sighed. "Oh, everything's getting so complicated! I really think we should obey that warning note," she said. "Mother seems much worse—I'm very much worried. I haven't told her about the note, but have hinted at the idea we should go away. Her health comes first. She simply won't leave. She keeps saying that my father entrusted his project to us, and she just won't abandon it."

Suddenly Elise said, "I'm sure it'll do Mother a lot of good to see you all."

Elise ran upstairs, and came down in a short time to say that Mrs. Hilary had consented to seeing the callers.

Louise, Jean, and Aunt Harriet followed their friend to Mrs. Hilary's attractive bedroom. The widow was seated in an overstuffed armchair. She wore a dressing gown and slippers, and, after she had greeted the Danas, apologized for her appearance.

Mrs. Hilary looked like an older edition of Elise, but was extremely thin and frail. Her beautiful blue eyes lost their sad expression and lighted up with real pleasure.

"I'm so glad to see you," she said warmly to her visitors. "It's been a long time. Since returning to Oak Falls I haven't really wanted to see anyone, but I know that's the wrong attitude. Still—until I feel better, I think it best if I remain quiet."

No mention was made of the mystery nor what had been happening in Oak Falls the past few weeks. Instead, talk turned to Elise's engagement. Louise told the Hilarys that the three Danas had an appointment with Mr. Archer for Saturday morning.

"Oh, that's wonderful!" Elise exclaimed. "I'm sure if anybody can do anything with him, you girls can."

After a few minutes of further conversation Louise caught a signal from her aunt that she wanted the three girls to go downstairs—presumably so that she might talk alone with Mrs. Hilary. Louise stood up, saying she thought they had stayed long enough. She said good-bye and led the way from the room. After the girls reached the first floor, she explained Miss Dana's signal to Jean and Elise.

"Oh, I know your Aunt Harriet can help Mother," Elise declared.

At that moment the doorbell rang. The caller was Keith Bartlett. He was cordial in his greetings, but the Danas immediately noticed a worried expression in his eyes.

"I just had to come over here," he said. "I'm so fed up with that newspaper office I could go out and tackle a couple of bulls!"

The girls begged him to explain. At once he launched into the subject on his mind.

"A story came to the paper a short time ago that the black-robed ghost pulled another one of his scares. This time it was serious. An elderly couple had been walking along one of the more secluded streets in town. A figure wearing black rushed up to them and started to drag the woman away. Her husband fought off the ghost, who finally turned and fled.

"Unfortunately," Keith continued, "the poor man had a heart attack and was taken to the hospital."

"How dreadful!" Elise gasped.

The Danas, too, expressed their horror, then Jean asked, "Did the couple get a good look at their assailant?"

"No. The stranger's face was hidden by a black hood."

Keith Bartlett went on to say that he had tried his best to have only a brief account of the incident printed, and keep it off the front page. However, he had been vetoed by the editor, Farley. "I called

Mr. Archer on the telephone to discuss it with him, but couldn't reach him."

"Do you think," Louise asked, "that Mr. Farley feels he owes it to the public to give every detail of the story?"

"No, I don't. In this particular case, I frankly believe he is being influenced by those two men who want to buy the paper. I figure they've told him if they take charge, he will stay on at an increased salary—if he plays along with them."

"And I suppose," said Elise, frowning, "that because *you* don't agree, you'd lose your job."

"Exactly."

Elise told her fiancé of the appointment which Louise, Jean, and their aunt had with Mr. Archer. Jean laughed. "We'll do the best we can for you, Keith."

"I appreciate that. But you'll find Mr. Archer a tough nut to crack."

At that moment Miss Dana came downstairs. She and Keith were introduced, and after a brief chat, the Danas left. As they returned to their own home, Aunt Harriet told Jean and Louise that Mrs. Hilary had begged her to come and stay at the cottage.

"In fact, she wants all three of us to stay," Aunt Harriet went on. "She seems to think that she and Elise will feel better if we're there."

"That's very flattering," said Jean. "I'd love to go!"

"We'll have to wait a few days," Aunt Harriet explained, smiling. "I have a surprise—your Uncle Ned is due home tomorrow afternoon."

"Hurray!" Jean exclaimed.

"Oh, that's wonderful!" said Louise. "It's been ages since we've seen Uncle Ned."

When they reached the Dana home, Aunt Harriet frowned. "I thought we left the front hall light on," she commented.

"We did," said Louise. "The bulb must have burned out."

They went up the front steps and Aunt Harriet handed the key to Louise. She unlocked the door and stepped inside to test the light. As she lifted her hand to do so, the Danas heard a low-throated growl. The next moment a vicious, unseen animal jumped onto Louise. She screamed in pain as his teeth sank into her arm!

CHAPTER IX

The Man Called Abdul

"Oh, GRACIOUS! Louise!" cried Aunt Harriet, panic-stricken, and pushed into the hallway.

Jean quickly reached for the light switch. Instantly the hallway was brightly illuminated.

Standing back a little distance from the Danas and yelping wildly was a mongrel with a definite trace of bloodhound. A long rope, tied around the dog's neck, was fastened to the newel of the stairway. He was tearing at the rope with his teeth.

Louise had taken refuge in the living room. Jean and Aunt Harriet, greatly concerned, followed her.

"Louise, did he bite you?" Aunt Harriet asked worriedly.

By this time Louise had removed her coat and rolled up the sleeve of her dress. "Here are the teeth marks, but he didn't break the skin, thank goodness."

Now that the others knew the animal's attack on Louise had not been serious, the three Danas excitedly speculated on who had brought the dog into the house and why. Was the reason merely to frighten them again? Or was there a more sinister motive? And how had the intruder gained admittance?

Jean went to inspect the various windows and the rear door. Presently she called, "Someone forced the back-door lock!"

Louise and Aunt Harriet went to look. Miss Dana remarked, "I suppose it was the same person who was here before. When he didn't find the key hidden behind the shutter, he decided to break in."

"But why?" Jean insisted. "We know now that he isn't a thief. What *is* his purpose in coming?"

Louise said she was convinced it was to keep the sisters from working on the Hilary case.

"What are we going to do with this animal— call the police?" Aunt Harriet asked.

"I have another idea," Jean replied. "If we can calm the dog and take him outside, he'll probably lead us to his owner. That may help solve the case."

The others agreed this was logical reasoning. But the question was, could they control the agitated dog?

"Food often does wonders," said Aunt Harriet. "Why don't we try that first?"

She went to the refrigerator and brought out

what was left of a roast beef which the family had had for dinner. She cut off chunks of the tender meat and put them in a bowl.

"There's some cooked oatmeal on the second shelf of the refrigerator," Miss Dana said. "Jean, suppose you mix that with the meat."

While this was being done, Louise got another bowl and filled it with water. Then the Danas went back to the front hall and placed the bowls on the floor. The dog, sniffing the meat, quieted at once and began to gobble the food hungrily.

As the girls and their aunt watched him, they felt sure that the viciousness he had shown in the beginning was entirely due to fear. Now that he could trust his benefactors, Louise pointed out, the animal probably would be quite docile. This proved to be the case. When the dog finished eating, he lay down with his head between his front paws and gazed in a friendly way at the Danas. Finally Louise walked up to him slowly, holding out her hand.

"You didn't mean to hurt me, did you?" she said. "You're a nice old fellow, and we're going to take you home tomorrow morning."

This time the dog licked her hand and wagged his tail. Louise laughed. "You poor thing! The idea of anyone's bringing you here and tying you up in the dark!"

About an hour later the dog readily accompanied the sisters outside for a short walk. He made no attempt to break away and willingly came back into the house with them. At once the mystery animal lay down in the hall.

Later, as Louise and Jean got ready for bed, Jean suddenly giggled. "We'd better be sure we're downstairs tomorrow before Applecore arrives. If that dog should go after her, she'd panic, and Aunt Harriet would be minus a maid."

The following morning when Cora arrived, the girls were on hand to introduce the animal to her. Warily, she kept a safe distance from him. When she heard of his mysterious arrival, Cora threw her hands up and wailed.

"The b-black-robed ghost's been here again! Oh, I'll die if I stay in this house!"

Aunt Harriet then told Cora the family's plan to visit the Hilarys for a short time. "Also, Captain Dana will be home this afternoon, so I'm sure you'll feel safer."

"Thank goodness! That's the best news I've heard in a long time!" Cora said emphatically.

Directly after breakfast, the girls put on plaid flannel slacks and car coats with hoods, took the dog on the rope, and let him lead the way. Part of the time they had to run to keep up with his eager pace.

Finally Louise called a halt. "I'm out of breath!" she admitted. "I wonder if this dog is really going to take us to his master or whether he's only playing games?"

"There's no way of knowing yet," Jean replied. "I guess we'll just have to keep going."

After a short rest the trio started out again. Soon they found themselves on one of the country roads leading out of Oak Falls. As they went along, the animal suddenly tugged hard at the rope and began to leap ahead.

"Whoa there!" cried Jean, who was holding him.

She managed to slow him down a bit, but Louise said excitedly, "I'm sure he knows now where he's going!"

Five minutes later the animal turned abruptly into a lane which led to a farmhouse. He began to bark loudly. Two small boys who were playing in the yard turned around, then ran towards the callers.

"Mickey! Mickey!" they cried out happily.

As soon as they reached the dog, the boys began to hug him and he in turn whined and wagged his tail furiously.

Finally the two lads looked up at the sisters. One of them asked, "Where's the man who took Mickey away?"

The girls smiled. "We don't know," Louise replied. "Mickey was left at our house and we let him find his own way home. Is your mother here?"

"Yes. I'll get her," said the other child.

He ran into the house and in a minute emerged with a woman in her early thirties. She was rather stout and had a large quantity of blonde hair wound in a knot on top of her head.

"Mama, these girls brought Mickey back," the older child explained. "He got left at their house."

"I don't understand," said the boys' mother to the girls. "I'm Mrs. McGregor. This is Joey, and the little fellow is Johnny."

Louise nodded towards the children and said, "Mrs. McGregor, do you mind if we come inside and talk? Maybe Joey and Johnny would like to play with Mickey out here."

The woman led the way into the house. Seeing that the girls looked rather weary, she offered them some soda. As they were drinking it, Louise and Jean took turns relating what had happened at their home the night before.

Mrs. McGregor was aghast. "Oh, gracious! You don't think *we* had anything to do with that, do you?"

"No," Louise replied. "But can you tell us how or why it happened?"

Mrs. McGregor explained that the previous afternoon a man calling himself Mr. Abdul had come to the farmhouse. "He seemed like a real gentleman—spoke with a British accent," she went on. "He said he wanted to borrow our dog for a few hours while he went walking in the woods. He offered me ten dollars for the privilege." The children's mother sighed. "We sometimes do rent

Mickey to hunters, since we need the extra money, so I agreed."

"Will you describe this Mr. Abdul?" Jean asked.

Mrs. McGregor said he was tall, slender, swarthy, and had piercing eyes. "Kind of handsome in a way," she added. "But I guess he wasn't a gentleman after all. Can I do anything to help you find him?"

Louise had a sudden idea. "Your dog has some bloodhound in him. Perhaps if he had a scent to go by, he could trace Mr. Abdul for us."

"Mr. Abdul didn't leave anything here that the dog could smell," said the woman. "Maybe Mickey could pick up his footprints, though. The man went in that direction." She pointed towards the road and a wooded hillside beyond it.

"Do you still have the ten dollars he gave you?" Louise asked.

"Yes, I do. You think maybe the scent of his hands is on it?"

Louise nodded. Mrs. McGregor went to a cupboard drawer for the money.

"By the way, do you have a collar and leash for Mickey?" Jean asked.

Mrs. McGregor said that Mr. Abdul had taken the good ones. "He must have taken them off to avoid identification. I do have an old leash and collar which I guess will do." She went to get them.

The three walked outdoors and the collar and

leash were fastened to Mickey. Meanwhile, Louise
let the animal sniff the ten-dollar bill. Finally she
dragged it across the ground, with the dog following her. Suddenly he seemed to realize what was
wanted of him and started to bound down the lane.

Louise and Jean could hardly keep up with the
dog's swift pace. He sniffed along the side of the
road for about half a mile, then set off across a field.

"Mickey's heading for those woods," said Louise.
"Maybe Mr. Abdul was telling the truth and really
did take a stroll. It's just possible that the dog
was stolen from him and put in our house by someone else."

Jean giggled, saying, "You're a trusting soul,
Louise—*I* have a definite feeling Mr. Abdul is one
of the people connected with the Oak Falls mystery, and the sooner we locate him, the better!"

"Perhaps. But I doubt if we're going to find him
in these woods," said Louise. "When I suggested
trying to follow his scent, I thought Mickey probably would take us back to town."

The dog was straining hard at the leash, apparently enjoying his task. It occurred to both girls
that Mr. Abdul was not a "gentleman." He might
have mistreated Mickey—whose eagerness could
mean a desire for revenge.

The girls stumbled along after the animal—over
ruts, hummocks, and soggy spots in the field and
through masses of thistles which tore at their slacks.

Finally Mickey dashed straight into the thick,

dense woods. He became even more excited and began to bark.

Suddenly Louise caught her breath and grabbed Jean's arm. "Stop!" she cried out.

Jean halted so suddenly that the dog almost did a somersault. Then Jean saw why her sister had cried out. She could not believe her eyes.

Several yards away, emerging from a thicket, was a fierce-looking striped tiger! The powerful beast began to roar as it stalked menacingly towards the girls!

CHAPTER X

A Strange Disappearance

JEAN and Louise did an about-face, yanking the dog after them. They raced pell-mell from the woods and did not glance back until they were in the field. They stopped for breath but kept a wary watch for any sign of the tiger.

Finally Jean panted, "The story is true! A tiger *is* roaming the woods of Oak Falls!"

Louise nodded. "And we'd better get out of here fast and report it to the police!"

Looking around, the girls spotted a road at the far end of the field and a bus speeding along it. They hurried over and sat down to wait for the next bus. Finally it arrived and Louise signalled the driver. He slowed but would not let them board, calling out:

"No dogs allowed!"

As the bus went on, the sisters stared after it in

dismay. They were afraid to hail a passenger car because of the strange happenings around town. Finally they decided to walk back to the farmhouse, and set off across the field with Mickey. At the farm, the girls whispered a warning to Mrs. McGregor about the tiger. The woman paled, but said nothing lest her children become panicky. The dog was left with his owners, then the Danas took a bus back to their own house.

Aunt Harriet was horrified to hear there was a tiger in the neighbourhood and offered to phone headquarters to report the incident. When she rejoined her nieces in the living room, Louise was stretched out on the couch and Jean lay on the floor with a pillow under her head.

Miss Dana smiled understandingly, then said, "I have news too. The insurance adjuster was here about the car. The damage isn't extensive."

"What!" cried Louise, sitting bolt upright. "Why, Emil Gifford said—I'm going to call Irving's Auto Repair Service and find out about this!"

She jumped up from the couch and went to the hall telephone. After a lengthy conversation with the garage owner, Louise announced:

"Emil Gifford has suddenly disappeared!"

"Disappeared!" Jean echoed.

"He has not only left his job," her sister replied, "but he has left town, taking money from Mr. Irving's cash register."

"I wonder if he had any other reasons for leaving than just robbing Mr. Irving?" Aunt Harriet speculated.

Louise said she had more news. Mr. Irving had expressed surprise at not having heard from the Danas about repairing the car. "The damage to the body and gear shift can be fixed quickly."

Jean's eyes narrowed thoughtfully. "Emil Gifford must be shrewder than we realized. I'll bet he had a reason for making up that story about our car."

"Could be," Louise agreed. "Maybe Emil wanted to keep track of our activities connected with the Oak Falls mystery. Oh, I know it's a guess, but— it *is* strange how he popped up a few days before the accident."

"Exactly!" Jean cried excitedly. "In fact, I wouldn't be surprised if Emil himself is mixed up in the ghost mystery and didn't want us working on it."

Aunt Harriet looked disturbed. "You mean that if you did not have a car, you'd be more apt to walk or, as he hoped, phone him for a ride—so he would know your destination?"

"Yes!" Louise responded. "And when he found we were determined, and getting near the truth, Emil decided to disappear."

Miss Dana thought this reasoning was a little far-fetched, but she had learned from experience that her nieces' hunches were more often right than wrong. "Do you suppose," she asked, "Emil Gifford might have put that horrible mask in our window and left the snake and turban?"

"Anything's possible at this point," Jean said. "Maybe Emil left the dog here. If so, he must be connected in some way with Mr. Abdul."

Miss Dana remarked that the name Abdul and the description the girls had of him from Mrs. McGregor indicated he might be from India. "The educated Indians speak English with a British accent."

Jean was excited about all these new angles. "Louise, let's go right over to Emil Gifford's house and see what we can find out from his wife."

She called Irving's repair shop to obtain Emil's address. The sisters then caught a bus and soon were ringing the bell of a house in a rather run-down neighbourhood. There was no answer. Disappointed, the Danas started to leave.

At that moment Jean noticed a woman clipping a barberry hedge nearby. She hurried over and asked her how to get in touch with Mrs. Gifford.

"I wouldn't know," the neighbour replied. "The Giffords—and their car—have disappeared into thin air—nobody seems to know where they went, and nobody particularly cares. They're kind of noisy folks."

Louise joined her sister. Jean thanked the neighbour and the two girls walked away. Then Louise stopped. "Jean, what's the name of the friend who went with Mrs. Gifford to the museum?"

"I think it's Crocker."

Jean turned back and spoke to the woman who was vigorously clipping the hedge once more. "I'm sorry to bother you again, but do you happen to know where Mrs. Crocker lives?"

"Forty-two Wabash Street."

Jean again thanked the woman, and the sisters hurried off. They found Mrs. Crocker to be a pleasant person, but as soon as they mentioned Mrs. Gifford's name, a hurt expression came over her face.

"I have no idea where Grace and her husband are," she said. "I feel bad that she did not tell me her plans. We're very close friends."

Now that Mrs. Crocker had started talking, it seemed as if she were glad to unburden her mind. "Grace and I were schoolmates. Everything was fine until she married Emil. I never liked him and her parents didn't either. It wouldn't surprise me," she confided, "if Grace and Emil have parted and she's gone home to her family."

"But that doesn't explain *Mr.* Gifford's disappearance," said Louise. "Have you any idea why he might have left without telling anyone?"

"I can only guess," said Mrs. Crocker. "I know Emil owed everybody in town—he was always spending beyond his means. It was pretty hard on Grace. She tried to cover up for him, but maybe this time she couldn't stand it any more."

Jean asked where Mrs. Gifford's parents lived. The answer was discouraging. "I'm not sure, but I *think* they went to live in Florida. Lately Grace has become rather secretive. I felt sorry for her, so I didn't ask about her troubles—but I kept hoping she'd tell me on her own."

Since there was nothing more to be learned from Mrs. Crocker, the Danas thanked her and left. When they reached the main street of Oak Falls, Louise suddenly began to run. "Hurry, Jean! We must catch that bus!"

Jean dashed after her sister, but wondered what was on her mind. The bus was going in the direction opposite to their home!

When they were aboard, Louise, out of breath, laughed. "I just remembered about Uncle Ned. We'll have a little time to do some sleuthing at the airport before his plane arrives."

Jean nodded. "By sleuthing I suppose you mean inquiring at the various airline counters if a Mr. and Mrs. Emil Gifford flew out of here—and when."

"You guessed it!"

The girls' inquiries, however, yielded no clue. So far as they could learn, the Giffords had not left town by plane.

"Perhaps they didn't go together," Louise said. "One may have taken a bus and the other their car."

Jean smiled. "It could be we've seen the last of Emil. If so, some of the strange happenings in Oak Falls may end."

Louise said she doubted it. "There's still a certain Mr. Abdul to consider!"

There was no more time for speculation, since Uncle Ned's plane was landing. The girls went to the gate to meet him. They felt a surge of joy as they saw the handsome grey-haired man descend the steps from the aircraft. He was large in build, and rugged looking, with a merry twinkle in his keen blue eyes.

"Uncle Ned!" shouted Louise and Jean.

A moment later he had encircled both girls with his arms. "Well, my hearties, you didn't fail me! You came down to my airship. She docked right on time, too."

The sisters laughed. Their uncle was truly a skipper on dry land as well as on the sea!

As the three walked towards a taxi, he remarked how well his nieces looked. "I guess your gadding about all over our great West hasn't hurt you one bit," he said.

"It agrees with us," Jean assured him gaily.

As soon as Uncle Ned had greeted Aunt Harriet and Cora, the captain inquired about his nieces' activities since returning to Oak Falls. His eyes twinkling more than ever, he said, "I'd like to bet you're both in the midst of another mystery."

"A *terrible* mystery with a *ghost* in it," put in

Cora, whose admiration for Captain Dana was unbounded. "This house is almost haunted! We got mad dogs, and burglars, and snakes, and everything!"

Uncle Ned looked dumfounded. His sister and the girls, amused, let Cora tell what had happened. She distorted the story so badly that the captain took a long breath and appealed to the others to "straighten him out." After hearing the full and correct story, he became serious.

"I think Cora is right in not taking this matter lightly," he said, frowning. "The person or persons who are in back of this whole thing are bad actors. I wish you girls weren't mixed up in it. In fact—" He paused and looked at his nieces intently.

Louise and Jean exchanged fearful glances. Was Uncle Ned about to forbid them to continue their detecting?

CHAPTER XI

Abductor's Footprints

WORRIEDLY, the Dana sisters waited for their uncle's next words. To their great relief, he merely said, "In a way I'll be glad when you're back in school and away from this haunted town."

Impishly Jean spoke up. "We have enough time left to solve the mystery before we go!"

Uncle Ned smiled and shook his head. Just then the doorbell rang. Cora went to see who was there and returned carrying a special-delivery letter for Jean addressed on a typewriter. At first she thought it must be from Chris, but then she noticed the postmark—Oak Falls. Curious, she tore open the envelope.

"Another letter for Elise!" she exclaimed, taking out an enclosed envelope.

Her uncle wanted to know why the letter had not been sent direct to Elise.

"We think," Jean replied, "that perhaps the

writer wants us to know the contents and hopes to scare us off the mystery."

Jean telephoned Elise and made a date to visit her after supper. When she announced this to her family, Uncle Ned said at once, "I'll go along. I don't want either of you girls on the streets alone at night."

It was decided that Louise would stay at home with Aunt Harriet while Jean and Uncle Ned called on Elise.

When they reached the cottage that evening, Jean anxiously waited to hear the contents of the note. After Elise had read it, she exclaimed, "Oh dear! More trouble!"

"Another warning?" Jean asked.

"Yes—and this threat is worse than the first! It says:

" 'Do not marry Bartlett. Stars are not in right position. Unhappiness and tragedy will follow if you disobey the signs in the heavens.' "

When she finished, there was complete silence for several seconds. Then Captain Dana asked, "Have you any idea who sent this, Elise?"

"No. But it's someone familiar with an old, superstitious custom in India. It's still practiced by some astrologers who make predictions by the positions of the stars."

Elise went on to say that before a marriage contract was arranged, the horoscopes of the bride-to-be and her fiancé had to be consulted.

"It is believed by many Indians that during part of everyone's life a bad star is in evidence. During that time accidents, death, or an unfortunate marriage will take place."

"And those superstitious people plan their lives according to all this?" Jean asked.

"Yes, indeed," Elise replied. "These astrologers —and many of them are fakers—earn a living by their profits from such predictions."

Captain Dana asked Elise if she thought the note might have been written by an Indian astrologer. "Personally," he answered himself, "I don't believe it was. Somebody has used this method to scare you. Perhaps he thinks because you lived in India for a while you might have come to believe this superstition."

"Well if so, he's absolutely wrong!" Elise declared. "Keith and I intend to be married. Oh, I hope Mr. Archer can be convinced that he should sell the *News* to Keith."

"I like your spirit!" said Captain Dana. "Just because you're travelling on rough seas is no reason for abandoning ship!" The remark cheered Elise immensely.

Soon afterwards the two Danas left. Uncle Ned said to Jean, "Look at that sky! Beautiful clouds, a bright moon, and those stars"—he laughed softly —"all good stars! What say we walk home?"

"Wonderful idea! Let's go by way of the museum. I'd like to show you the stone tiger."

"And I'd like to see it," said Captain Dana.

Jean led the way to the front of the museum. The two stopped and the captain gazed in awe at the statue. "It's magnificent," he said, and walked up close to the tiger.

Jean did not move. Was it her imagination or had she heard a light footstep somewhere behind them? As she turned to look, a strong hand was suddenly clapped over her mouth and a covering placed tightly around her head. Jean kicked violently, but the next instant she was carried off!

Captain Dana, hearing running footsteps, looked around. To his great astonishment, Jean had disappeared! Suddenly he caught sight of a black-robed figure carrying someone who was struggling violently.

"Jean!" gasped the captain.

The figure was disappearing around the side of the museum.

The captain started off in pursuit but at this moment the moon was hidden by a cloud and he found it difficult to make his way forward with any speed.

"Jean will be gone before I can rescue her!" he moaned.

Just then the bright headlights of an approaching car illuminated the scene. The instant before the car turned the corner onto Madison Street, Captain Dana glimpsed the black-robed figure racing across the estate lawn in the direction of Snowden Drive.

Uncle Ned put on a burst of speed, but tripped over a tree root and went sprawling to the ground.

The car stopped in front of the museum. Two police officers jumped out. They beamed flashlights ahead of them as they came up the path.

Uncle Ned quickly got to his feet and ran towards the policemen. "Over this way!" he shouted. "The ghost has carried off my niece!"

The officers did not pause to question him. Sweeping their lights from left to right, they sprinted across the grounds in the direction the captain indicated. Uncle Ned followed.

Suddenly he stopped and exclaimed, "There she is—on the ground!"

Jean lay struggling to free her head from the tightly wound scarf. Just as the men reached her, she managed to tear off the heavy cloth.

"Thank goodness you're all right!" said Uncle Ned, helping Jean to her feet. "Where did that ghostly figure go?"

As soon as Jean caught her breath she replied, "I don't know. I guess he got scared when you began chasing him. Anyhow, he dropped me all of a sudden."

The policemen, meanwhile, had run to Snowden Drive. They peered up and down the street and checked the shrubbery, but found no one. They returned to the Danas.

"Tell us what happened." Jean now recognized the speaker as Sergeant Renley. When he heard the story, the officer said, "I'll radio a report to head-quarters at once. It seems pretty evident you Danas are targets of this mysterious ghost. I wonder where the scoundrel would have taken you."

Jean gave a shudder, but smiled wanly. "I have no idea. I'm glad you got here!"

"I only wish I could have caught that fellow," Captain Dana said grimly. "Did he say anything to you, Jean?"

"Oh, I almost forgot! And it's an important clue, too," his niece replied. "He warned me that if the Danas didn't stop meddling, no one would be safe."

"Any clue to his identity?" asked the sergeant.

Jean answered with satisfaction. "Yes. He had a British accent. I believe he may be the man calling himself Mr. Abdul, who paid ten dollars to borrow the McGregors' dog Mickey."

Sergeant Renley looked admiringly at the young detective. "Excellent clue," he said. "I'll add it to my report. Our men ought to pick up this Mr. Abdul in short order."

The group walked out to the police car and Sergeant Renley offered to take the Danas home. They accepted gratefully. As soon as he had reported to headquarters, the sergeant started the motor and in a few minutes had the Danas back at their own home.

"Please let us know as soon as you catch Mr. Abdul," said Jean, and thanked the sergeant and his companion for helping to rescue her.

When Louise and Aunt Harriet heard of Jean's experience, they were furious. "The idea of trying to kidnap you!" Miss Dana cried.

Louise said, "At least the net seems to be closing around Mr. Abdul. I have no doubt now that he's the mysterious black-robed ghost."

"And I'm sure those woods we were in have something to do with his scheme," Jean declared. "Speaking of the woods, I'll call headquarters in the morning and see if they've found out anything about the tiger."

The following day, however, when she put the question to the captain on duty, he told her that once more a search had been made in the West Woods. No tiger had been spotted.

"But my sister and I saw the animal," she insisted. "It must have been taken away by someone."

In discussing the tiger with their family, the sisters were surprised to have Uncle Ned say suddenly, "Did it ever occur to you that the tiger you saw might be a fake?"

The sisters looked startled. "It certainly looked real," said Jean. "And it was growling like those I've seen and heard in zoos."

Captain Dana went on, "Nowadays wild-animal costumes and tape recordings are made so cleverly that people can fit inside and play the part convincingly—as long as the whole figure of the beast isn't seen at one time."

Louise laughed. "You're probably right, Uncle

Ned. I never thought of that. But the tiger, whether real or artificial, is in those woods to keep people away. The question is, what can there be in them that one or more persons doesn't want seen?"

Aunt Harriet chuckled and said she knew there was no necessity of her asking the girls not to go sleuthing in the woods again—she was sure they did not wish a second tiger fright! "And now that we know the black-gowned ghost *will* resort to abduction, you girls had better be more wary than ever in your sleuthing."

Jean giggled. "I can laugh about it now, but I admit I really did have a bad scare last night."

Louise declared that nothing was going to deter her from trying to solve the mystery. "Let's go over to the museum, Jean, and see if we can pick up anything to identify your assailant."

Her sister agreed eagerly, so by nine o'clock they started out. On the museum grounds they picked up the footprints of a man, who, the girls assumed, was playing the part of the black-robed ghost. They followed the prints to a hedge that ran from Snowden Drive to a flower garden covered with fallen leaves. Here the prints ended.

"Now what?" Jean asked. "Did the ghost walk so lightly to the road that he left no more prints?"

"My guess is he jumped the hedge," her sister remarked. "Let's find out."

This proved to be true. The Danas spotted the same footmarks. They led towards Snowden

Drive and within a few yards were joined by a second set of prints.

"Another man met him!" Jean exclaimed.

Excitedly the two girls continued to follow the footprints. The indentations grew deeper, indicating that the two men had begun to run.

"They probably escaped in a car that was either standing at the curb or cruising—ready to pick them up," Jean deduced.

The girls were within thirty feet of the street when Louise suddenly cried out and pointed to the opposite side. "Look! That man in the car parked over there!"

CHAPTER XII

Tiger Hunt!

STARTLED, Louise gasped, "The driver of that car looks like Emil Gifford!"

The man apparently recognized the Dana girls, and stepped on the accelerator. His automobile roared off down the street.

"Oh, if only we had our car!" Jean groaned.

"Of course I'm not positive that was Emil," Louise pointed out. "But he certainly resembles him."

"The man certainly took off in a hurry," Jean pointed out. "That could mean he's guilty."

Both girls had noticed the licence number and memorized it. Louise suggested that they go inside the Hilary Museum and phone Irving's Auto Repair Service.

"We'll ask Mr. Irving if that is Emil's number," she said, "and also if he knows whether or not his mechanic is back in Oak Falls."

They rang the bell and Mr. Pryor admitted them, greeting the sisters cordially.

"I'd like to use your phone if I may," Louise said quickly.

"Help yourself."

She hurried to the hall table and dialled. When she spoke to Mr. Irving he was amazed to hear that Emil Gifford might be in town. "I can't remember his entire licence number, but the one you just mentioned sounds like it."

The garage owner then burst into a tirade against his former employee, and ended by saying, "He'd better come around here and repay the money he took from the cash register. If he thinks he's going to get away with that, he's mistaken!"

Louise learned that Mr. Irving had called the police to notify them of Emil Gifford's disappearance and to request that a search be made. "We'd like to talk to Emil ourselves," the young detective said.

"I'll let you know if the police find him," Mr. Irving promised. "By the way, your car is ready. When will you come for it?"

Louise said she and her sister would stop at the garage on their way home. "We'll certainly be glad to have our car again," she added. "We've been lost without it."

When Louise returned to Jean and Mr. Pryor, she found them discussing the mystery surrounding the Hilarys.

"I've been double-checking the doors and windows every night before I leave," the curator told the girls. "Besides, the police have been patrolling here more often. Maybe that black-robed ghost—or whoever the museum intruder is—will give up."

Louise and Jean secretly did not agree, but made no comment. Mr. Pryor went on bemoaning the fact that museum attendance remained at a standstill. "If that mysterious person was trying to discourage people from coming here, he certainly succeeded."

"What a shame!" Louise remarked, thinking that it would not be long before the Hilarys would be forced to close the museum. It contained such a worthwhile and informative display she felt this would be a real loss to Oak Falls and the surrounding area.

As the sisters left the old mansion, Louise suggested that they stop at Elise's home.

When the young woman opened the door, she said, "Oh, I'm so glad you came! I'm terribly worried!"

"Has something else happened?" Louise asked, concerned.

Elise nodded. In a whisper she told the Danas that her mother's condition was worse. "I was up with her all night. In spite of the medicine the doctor left for her, she couldn't sleep and hasn't eaten anything since suppertime last evening. She acts dreadfully nervous. Louise and Jean, do you think your Aunt Harriet could come over again? I'm sure she'd do Mother a lot of good, and maybe it would last until you all come to stay."

"I'm sure Aunt Harriet would be happy to," Louise replied, and telephoned her aunt at once. Miss Dana readily agreed, saying she would be at the cottage in a little while.

"But," she added, "you girls *must* come home and stay with your Uncle Ned. You know he's leaving tomorrow."

"We'll be right home," Louise promised.

As the sisters left the estate, they met Aunt Harriet who had just stepped off the bus. She carried a brown paper bag, and told the girls that she was taking a jar of homemade broth to Mrs. Hilary. "There's nothing like good beef-and-vegetable broth to bring back one's strength," said Miss Dana.

Louise and Jean smiled, recalling how many times their aunt's delectable cooking had made them feel better. They said good-bye and went on to Irving's Auto Repair Service. When the Danas saw their car, they exclaimed with pleasure. "The old wagon looks like new!" Jean bubbled.

"You're a magician," Louise said happily. Then she became serious. "Did the police have any report on Emil Gifford?"

"None at all. But they're looking for him, be sure of that."

The girls drove home, and after putting the car

in the garage, entered the kitchen. Cora greeted them with a relieved smile.

"Thank goodness you're back," she said. "Your Uncle Ned brought some oysters and wants stew for lunch. I've never made oyster stew in my *life*. Besides, I don't want to touch those squashy little things. They're alive, you know!"

"So I understand," said Louise, repressing a grin. "If they weren't alive before the shells were opened, you couldn't eat them."

Cora at last succeeded in digging the oysters out of their shells and then sat looking at them blankly.

"How do you ki-kill them?" she asked, staring helplessly.

Louise and Jean could not help laughing. "You just did," said Louise. "Now melt some butter, pop in the oysters—letting them simmer, add milk and seasoning, cook slowly, and that's it!"

Cora gave a little cry of dismay. "Not me!" she said. "I got ironin' to do down cellar. You fix the oyster stew!"

Before Louise and Jean could say a word, the maid whipped open the cellar door, slamming it behind her, and dashed below. The sisters, giggling, prepared the stew and the rest of the luncheon. In low voices they told the episode about Cora and the oysters to Captain Dana, who chuckled heartily.

"Good thing that gal was never stranded on a desert island—she'd starve to death!"

As soon as the three finished eating, Jean said to her uncle, "Now that we have the car back, how about a ride? Would you like to see the woods where we met that tiger?"

"If that's where me hearties would like to be sailin' to," Uncle Ned answered. "We can imagine we're on a trip along the Ganges River."

The girls laughed, put on their coats, and soon the three Danas were travelling along the highway. Louise was at the wheel. When she came to the field from where the sisters had entered the woods with the dog, Mickey, she stopped.

"Want to scoot in and take a look, Uncle Ned?" she asked.

After a moment's consideration, the captain replied, "I've been through some rough seas and dangerous times. I guess one old tiger shouldn't keep me below decks!"

It was Uncle Ned's youthful spirits which particularly endeared him to his nieces. Being adventurous themselves, the girls liked nothing better than to be setting out on a dangerous mission with him.

Louise locked the car, put the keys in her handbag, and the three hurried across the field and plunged into the woods. They followed the trampled path they had been on before and soon came to the spot where they had seen the tiger.

"Here we are," said Louise, looking around. "But no growling beast to show you."

Uncle Ned chuckled. "I can't say I'm disappointed."

Suddenly Jean, who had stepped off the path, exclaimed, "This is strange!"

"What?" Louise asked.

Her sister pointed to one of the larger trees. Thrust into the trunk was a sculptor's chipping tool.

"That's very odd indeed." Captain Dana remarked. "Why would anyone have left such a tool here?"

His nieces shrugged, but their thoughts were whirling. Both of them recalled that Mr. Abdul had told Mrs. McGregor he was going for a walk in these woods. Was it possible he owned the chipping tool?

"Do you think," asked Jean, "that Mr. Abdul could be a sculptor?"

"He's mysterious enough to be *anything*," Louise replied.

Uncle Ned suggested that none of them touch the chipping tool but report it to the police. "It may have revealing fingerprints." The three Danas quickly returned home and reported their find to the authorities.

It was nearly suppertime before Aunt Harriet returned. Louise and Jean were helping Cora prepare the meal.

"How is Mrs. Hilary?" Louise asked her aunt.

"After we talked for a while, she seemed much more cheerful and alert," Miss Dana answered. "She begged us to come there as soon as we could. I told her we'd arrive some time the day after to-morrow."

Despite the many puzzles on the girls' minds, and the forthcoming call on Mr. Archer, the supper hour was a jolly one and the family spent a delightful evening together. They went to bed fairly late. Not long afterwards they were aroused by the ringing of the telephone.

Captain Dana and his nieces met in the second-floor hall, all intending to answer it. As they passed Aunt Harriet's door, they could hear her saying on her bedroom extension, "Hello! Who is it?"

There was a long pause. The next moment the others were surprised when Miss Dana opened her door and beckoned to them. She whispered:

"Come in and listen! It's something horrible!"

CHAPTER XIII

The Buried Curse

Mystified, Captain Dana and the girls tiptoed after Aunt Harriet to the telephone in her bedroom. From the receiver came a cacophony of eerie sounds. They seemed to be a mixture of weird flute music and wild-animal cries.

"What in thunderation is going on?" Uncle Ned whispered.

"Nobody has spoken yet," his sister replied in a low voice.

"Sounds like someone having a bad nightmare," Jean murmured.

Suddenly Louise dashed from the room and ran down into Uncle Ned's den. She snapped on the light, grabbed up the battery-powered tape recorder he kept there, and returned to Aunt Harriet's room. Placing the machine close to the telephone, she began to record the sounds still coming from the receiver. They might prove to be a clue in the mystery!

Chills went up and down the spines of the listeners as a hyena laughed, a lion roared, and a big cat, probably a tiger, spat and hissed. Then, abruptly, the sounds ceased. There were a few moments of dead silence as the family waited tensely. Finally they heard a clipped, British-accented voice command:

"Danas, stop prying or evil will befall you! A buried curse has been put on you because of your interference in the Oak Falls mystery!"

The listeners heard a click. Whoever had made the phone call had hung up. Louise shut off the tape recorder and the Danas stared at one another in stunned amazement.

Finally Jean said, "That voice might have been Mr. Abdul's!"

The others agreed. But why had he used the strange introduction to his warning?

"I never heard of a buried curse," said Louise. "Does anybody know what it is?"

No one did and it was decided they would have to wait until morning to find out. "It's past midnight," Aunt Harriet observed. "I think we'd better go back to bed."

Louise and Jean were so excited by this latest episode in the mystery that they could not fall asleep at once. For nearly half an hour they discussed the who, what, and why of the odd telephone call. They could not figure it out, but in any event, it was obvious the caller's purpose had been to discourage them from further work on the case.

Jean yawned. "One thing is sure—that man is afraid of us, Louise, which is flattering. We must be better sleuths than I gave us credit for!"

Louise answered sleepily. "Uh-huh! I can't wait for morning to come. Well, good night again."

All the Danas were up early and had breakfast in their bathrobes and slippers. They finished eating by seven-thirty.

"How do you propose finding out what a buried curse is?" Uncle Ned asked his nieces.

Louise said she had an idea. "It might be some kind of an Indian superstition. I'll phone Elise and ask her if she knows."

"Great!" said Jean. "Please call her right away— I'm terribly curious!"

"And *I'm* terribly worried about this whole thing," Aunt Harriet added.

Captain Dana gave a grunt, then in a stentorian voice declared, "Whoever this mysterious person may be, I believe he is a coward. Thieves and evildoers in general *are* cowards." He looked affectionately at his nieces. "I think me hearties here have got this rascal backed into a corner."

The girls smiled their appreciation and each gave him a resounding kiss. Then Louise went to the telephone. Elise answered, and when Louise put her question, the young woman gasped.

"Oh, Louise, I don't like this at all! A buried curse is a practice among superstitious natives of India. I have heard that there are many cases on record where people have cast an evil spell on someone and—it has worked!"

"Surely you don't believe such things?" Louise asked, astonished.

Elise replied that after living in India for some time, one got the feeling that all sorts of strange and unexplainable tricks were played on people's minds. "Some of the astrologers and soothsayers have great influence—almost like hypnotism."

"Do you think our unknown caller last night was trying to cast a spell on us?" Louise asked.

"I'm not sure what he had in mind," Elise answered. "I suggest that you look in your yard to see if there's a newly dug spot. The curse may be buried there."

"Buried in our yard?" Louise repeated.

Elise explained that one of the requirements of the curse was that it be placed near the dwelling of the person threatened.

"Please look and call me back," she requested anxiously.

Louise returned to the table and told her family what Elise had suggested.

"Let's go!" Jean urged.

"In our pyjamas and robes?" Aunt Harriet asked, raising her eyebrows.

Captain Dana chuckled. "What difference does

that make? If any so-called curse has been put on this house, the sooner we know what it is, the better we can deal with it!"

Though the morning was crisp, the Danas were too excited to notice the chill. They rushed pell-mell out the kitchen door and began searching in the backyard. Not far from the garage, Jean discovered a freshly dug patch of earth.

"Here it is!" she exclaimed excitedly, and dashed into the garage for a shovel.

The others gathered around her and watched breathlessly as she quickly began digging. Not far below the surface she unearthed two round objects. One was covered with dark hair, the other was blond. Carefully Jean lifted one in each hand and held them up. The onlookers cried out in astonishment.

The objects were two wax heads. They were stuck full of pins and rosebush thorns, but there was no mistaking their identity.

"Those faces are Louise's and Jean's!" Aunt Harriet exclaimed, horrified.

"I—I guess we've found the buried curse." Louise shuddered slightly.

Uncle Ned looked grim. "I'm going to call the police!" he said, and hurried into the house.

Miss Dana and her nieces now began to feel cold —partly because of the low temperature, partly because of the shock. They returned to the house, with Jean gingerly carrying the queer wax heads.

She set them on the kitchen table. At that moment the back doorbell rang and Aunt Harriet opened it to admit Cora Appel.

"Good morn—" The maid stopped short and stared ahead. Then Cora gave one of her outlandish screeches. Pointing at the heads on the table, she cried out, "Wh-what are those things?"

"See any resemblance?" Jean could not resist asking.

"It's you and your sister!" Cora cried out. "You don't have to tell me any more. I just know something terrible's going to happen to you!"

When it was explained that the wax likenesses had been found buried in the backyard, Cora began to walk in circles, wringing her hands.

"Now calm down!" Aunt Harriet begged her. "We're going to—" Miss Dana stopped speaking and began to sniff. "Something's burning!"

Automatically those in the kitchen turned towards the stove. In dismay they saw that Cora had set her handbag close to the teakettle under which there was a low flame. The leather bag was smoldering!

Louise, nearest the stove, grabbed the bag. Cora looked at it forlornly. "The bad luck's following me too!" she exclaimed, and burst into tears.

"I'll buy you another pocketbook," Aunt Harriet told the distraught girl. "And now suppose you take off your coat and hat and get to work."

Louise telephoned Elise Hilary and told her what

they had found. "I'm not surprised," Elise said. "That follows exactly the old Indian custom of burying curses. It's meant to cast an evil spell on those whose faces are wrought in wax."

The two girls continued to discuss the situation. Louise remarked, "I've thought all along that the person responsible for creating this mystery is looking for something. I believe he's afraid Jean and I will find it first. Well, I certainly would like to do that very thing!"

"And I hope you can," said Elise, "but do be careful. This person seems to be growing more dangerous."

In a short while two policemen arrived at the house. Since the girls and Aunt Harriet had gone upstairs to dress, Uncle Ned talked with the officers. He gave them the tape recording of the phone call, and the two wax heads. The men told Captain Dana that no Mr. Abdul had been found in or near town, but the man might be using an assumed name and moving from one spot to another. Also, no prints had been found on the chipping tool.

At nine-thirty the sisters and their aunt left the house to keep their appointment with Mr. Archer at the newspaper office. The minute the Danas were shown into his private office, Louise and Jean knew he would be difficult to convince. The *News* owner's manner was cold, and the girls were sure that any request they might make regarding Keith Bartlett would not receive a friendly response. They decided to leave the whole matter to Aunt Harriet, since Mr. Archer had smiled fleetingly at her.

Miss Dana now stepped forward. "Tom, you and I are very proud of Oak Falls," she said, in what her nieces thought were honeyed tones.

"I used to be," Mr. Archer answered shortly.

"Why not now?" Miss Dana pursued. "You have a fine reputation and have built up an excellent newspaper. You wouldn't want all this to change, surely?"

Mr. Archer frowned as if he were extremely annoyed, pounded the desk, and glared at his visitors.

"I want you to go away!" he shouted. "Leave me alone! What will Oak Falls care when I'm gone?" A crafty look came into his eyes. "But the more money I can get into my estate, the better for my heirs! Now go! I—I—I—"

Suddenly Mr. Archer toppled forward over his desk!

CHAPTER XIV

An Elusive Voice

FEARFUL that Mr. Archer's attack of illness might be fatal, Louise and Jean dashed around his desk to help him. They caught him just before he toppled to the floor. Carefully they lifted the stricken man to a couch.

Louise felt his pulse, then said, "It's pretty weak, but he's still alive."

Meanwhile, Miss Dana had rushed to the outer office and spoken to Mr. Archer's secretary, Miss Lawton. Quickly the young woman pulled open a desk drawer, took out a bottle of pills, and spilled one into the palm of her hand. A messenger boy, who had just delivered some papers, dashed into the hall, panic-stricken.

"Mr. Archer left these with me for just such an emergency." Miss Lawton hastened to a water cooler and filled a paper cup with water.

She ran into the other room, followed by Aunt Harriet. The secretary asked Louise to raise Mr. Archer's head. The young woman laid the pill under his tongue, then set the cup of water on a table beside him.

"As soon as he's able, he must drink this cold water," the secretary said.

"You're sure he'll be all right?" Louise asked. Miss Lawton looked amazed at the question, as if it had never occurred to her Mr. Archer would not survive the attack. But now she looked worried.

"Don't you think we'd better get a doctor?" Miss Dana spoke up.

At that moment Keith Bartlett hurried into the office. Word of Mr. Archer's attack had been spread quickly by the messenger.

"I came at once," Keith said, looking worriedly at the thin, pale form on the couch. "Has anyone called a doctor?"

The others shook their heads. Instantly Keith went to the telephone and summoned Dr. Harvey.

The secretary, relieved, left the room and closed the door. The Danas and Keith watched Mr. Archer carefully, taking his pulse every few minutes.

"We were in the midst of a conversation with Mr. Archer when he became angry and excited," Louise explained to Keith. "Then he collapsed."

"Sh-h!" Aunt Harriet whispered. "I think he's regaining consciousness."

Everyone watched the elderly man closely and in a few moments he opened his eyes. The first people he noticed were the Danas.

"You—you," he said weakly, "were—here—when—I—fainted."

"Yes," Miss Dana answered gently. "My nieces laid you on the couch."

Mr. Archer closed his eyes again and did not open them for about twenty seconds. When he did, he looked directly at Keith Bartlett.

"And you?" he asked. "Where were you?"

"I came in as soon as I heard you were ill," Keith replied. "I phoned for the doctor. He'll be here any minute."

"My medicine—" the ill man said anxiously.

"Your secretary has already given you a pill," Louise told him. "Now you're supposed to drink this water." With one hand she lifted his head and with the other held the cup. The elderly man drank thirstily.

Miss Lawton appeared with Dr. Harvey. The others left the room but waited in the secretary's office. The physician's examination did not take long, and he soon reappeared, announcing that Mr. Archer would be all right.

"Thank goodness!" Aunt Harriet said, taking a deep breath.

"All he needs is rest," the doctor added. "I'll take him home in my car."

Keith instantly volunteered to help. In a minute

or two the doctor and Keith came out supporting Mr. Archer. He was seemingly oblivious to everything going on about him.

The Danas followed the men to the street, and as soon as Mr. Archer had been driven off in the doctor's car, they hurried home. Uncle Ned was waiting for them.

"That was a short conference," he said. "Now we can drive to the airport without rushing."

"I'm sorry you can't have lunch with us," his sister said, "but I know you have to get back to New York City."

Captain Dana chuckled. "If I don't arrive aboard the *Balaska* on time, there'll be a heap of angry sea-going folks!"

Aunt Harriet said good-bye to him, then he and his nieces went to the car. On the way to the airport, the girls told Uncle Ned about Mr. Archer.

"His health certainly isn't good," the captain remarked somberly. "The sooner Mr. Archer sells his newspaper, the better for him. Did you have any luck trying to persuade him to let Keith Bartlett buy it?"

Jean shook her head. "He's a hard man to talk to. We didn't have a chance to say much before he collapsed."

"Too bad," said Uncle Ned. "But you never can tell about men like Archer—he might change his mind about Keith's offer when he feels better."

"I certainly hope so!" Louise declared.

When they reached the terminal building at the airport, the girls found many people milling around. Suddenly Louise's attention was drawn to a voice which seemed to cut through the babble. A man with a British accent was saying, "Good-bye. The instructions are being carried out."

She grabbed Jean's arm. "I just heard a man speak in the same voice as the one that gave us the strange warning on the phone!"

"Where is he?" Jean asked excitedly.

"I don't know. His voice was clear—yet he didn't seem to be close by."

"Let's hunt for him," Jean urged eagerly.

"But if it should be Mr. Abdul, how will we know him?" Louise argued.

Jean had an idea. "We'll go to every man who fits the description Mrs. McGregor gave us and find an excuse to make him speak."

Quickly Louise and Jean told Uncle Ned they were going on an errand but would be right back. He said he would wait on a nearby bench.

The girls separated, taking opposite directions. They peered at first one man, then another. Presently Jean approached one leaning against a telephone booth. In a general way he matched the description of Mr. Abdul.

"Excuse me. Are you going to use this booth?" Jean asked him.

The man's answer was so far from a cultured British voice that she almost laughed aloud. "Naw," he said. "Help yourself, miss," he replied in nasal tones.

Jean, instead of turning into the booth, walked off, leaving the man to stare after her, puzzled. A little later she spotted another person who fitted Abdul's description, and was just about to ask him a question, when she recognized the man. He owned a sporting-goods store in Oak Falls!

Louise had had no success either, and presently the two girls met again at the bench where Captain Dana was seated.

"Now tell me what you two have been up to," he demanded. "I saw you sailing around, looking at each and every man in this place!"

"Not every one!" Jean grinned and explained. "But we didn't have any luck."

"Perhaps the fellow hopped a plane," said Uncle Ned. "Well, me hearties, I guess I'll have to say good-bye now. Take care." His eyes crinkled into a smile. "If I hear anybody on my plane speaking like a Britisher, I'll find out if he's Mr. Abdul!"

The sisters each gave their uncle an affectionate farewell hug, and stood waving after him. Once the plane was air-borne, Louise and Jean decided to ask at each of the airline counters if a passenger named Abdul had recently purchased a ticket. The girls were told that Mr. Abdul had left on a New York flight a few hours earlier. He was already there.

Louise and Jean were intrigued by this information. They had at last gleaned a clue to their quarry!

"This is great," said Louise, as the sisters turned away. "But I'm stymied about that voice I heard. I'm *sure* I recognized it."

Jean had no solution except to suggest that the speaker had been in a telephone booth, and had left the terminal before the girls had begun their search.

Louise sighed. "I wish we could put the pieces of this puzzle together. Do you suppose that Mr. Abdul is actually still here, but wanted the police and us to think he left town? He might have had someone else take his place on the plane, using his name!"

CHAPTER XV

The Big Cat Speaks!

"IF THERE'S any likelihood of Mr. Abdul's still being in Oak Falls," said Louise to Jean, "what do you think our next move should be?"

"To tell our suspicions to the police."

"And then what?"

Jean thought for several seconds before answering. "I have a hunch that somehow the museum's stone tiger has a direct bearing on this mystery."

"That's right," Louise agreed. "And don't forget, we were told this mystery started soon after the statue was delivered to the Hilary estate."

Louise made the call to headquarters, then rejoined her sister. Jean offered a suggestion. "Why don't we go over to the museum and talk to Mr. Pryor? He can give us more information on tigers. Something may be a clue."

The Danas had a quick lunch, then left. The curator was very glad to see them. He seemed happy to have the chance to expound on tigers. "Well—the beasts subsist on mice, locusts, fish, and small animals," he began. "Unlike most members of the cat family, tigers are poor climbers."

"So if I were ever chased by one," said Jean, "my best bet would be to climb a tall tree?"

"Right." Mr. Pryor went on to say that tigers hunt by ear. "They have a very poor sense of smell —and poor vision."

Jean giggled. "You make it sound as if these terrors of the jungle aren't dangerous at all!"

Mr. Pryor smiled. "I wouldn't go so far as to say that. But it is not too hard for a human being or a wild animal to outwit the tiger."

Louise asked, "Who are their natural enemies?"

"Elephants, water buffalo, and dholes—mostly. By the way, the Indian dhole is exceedingly fierce and can't be tamed. I'd rather have a tiger after me any day than a dhole!"

Jean remarked that she would prefer her tigers in the form of statues. "Louise and I have been wondering whether or not your beautiful stone tiger could possibly be the cause of the Oak Falls mystery."

"How could it be?" the curator asked. "It has no value except as art."

The Dana girls said that they had never examined the statue closely, and would like to do so now. "Do you mind?" Louise asked.

"Not at all. I'll go with you," Mr. Pryor offered.

The three went outdoors and the two young detectives began to inspect the large stately stone cat. They marvelled at how perfectly the black veins in the marble represented the beast's stripes. Every detail of the carving was perfect.

"I guess there aren't any clues here," Mr. Pryor remarked finally.

Jean had turned away, but Louise was still studying the tiger. She bent down and turned her head so that she might look closely at the underside of the body. Raising her hand, she ran her fingers over the animal's chest.

Suddenly her eyes lighted up excitedly. "Somebody has been chipping at the tiger!" she announced.

"What!" Mr. Pryor exclaimed, rushing forward.

Jean, too, looked at the roughened surface. "You're right, Louise!" she exclaimed.

"But why?" the curator asked.

Louise suggested that perhaps the statue was hollow and that something valuable might be hidden inside.

"But the tiger is *solid!*" Mr. Pryor objected.

Louise and Jean glanced at each other, the same thought coming to their minds. Was the sculptor's chipping tool they had found in a tree of any significance? Could the person who had put it there be responsible for defacing the stone tiger, and was that person Mr. Abdul?

"Maybe there was another reason for someone

chipping the statue," Jean suggested. "Some superstitious reason, for instance."

Mr. Pryor became thoughtful. He remarked that he felt personally responsible for protecting the statue. He still could not understand, however, why anyone should tamper with the marble. "It's just possible that no one noticed previously that this section of the statue had not been smoothly finished."

At that moment Jean and Louise noticed two men coming up the path. They were young, of medium height, and both were grinning.

"You have visitors," Louise told the curator.

"At last!" Mr. Pryor said happily.

When the two young men reached the museum, the curator introduced himself and then led them inside. The three had been gone scarcely three minutes when the curator returned to the front door and called the girls.

"Please come in," he requested. "These men are reporters from New York City, and insist upon having the complete story of everything that has happened here at the museum and in town. They're convinced there's more to it than appeared in our *News*."

Louise and Jean could see that Mr. Pryor was very nervous. They were sure that he did not want to reveal anything which would further embarrass and upset the Hilary family. He introduced the

girls to the men and explained that they were ama-
teur detectives.

"Glad to meet you," said one of the visitors.
"I'm Bill McCaffrey and this is my pal Joe Steele."

Joe looked at the sisters in amusement. "*You* are
trying to solve a mystery that's baffling the *police?*"

The sisters bristled inwardly at the question.
They decided on the spot to tell the reporters nothing of importance. Louise coolly countered with,
"Did you come all the way up here from New York
for a silly small-town tale?"

The men blinked. Obviously they had not expected such a response.

"So you're going to give us the run-around?"
Joe said.

His friend interrupted brusquely. "Let's stop this
nonsense and get down to business. Now, Mr.
Pryor, when did you first notice anything mysterious happening at the museum?"

The curator replied slowly, "I can't remember
the exact date. Somebody got in here and disturbed
things a bit, that's all! But nothing was stolen."

Louise spoke up in a nonchalant tone. "Some
practical joker is loose in Oak Falls." She shrugged.
"Surely you men don't report every funny thing
that happens on Halloween! You'd better put this
whole story in the dead-end file."

"Anyway, we have reason to believe the mischief-maker has left town," Jean put in. She smiled

beguilingly. "So really, there *isn't* any story for you."

The reporters, again taken aback, were silent for several moments, then Joe Steele asked, "What's this mischief-maker's name?"

Jean, not to be caught off guard, replied, "Nobody knows. He's probably using aliases."

Bill McCaffrey, who had pulled out a notebook from his pocket, put it back in disgust. "I can see we're not going to get anything out of these people," he said to his companion. "We'll check other sources in town. Maybe someone else will be more cooperative."

The Danas were fearful that the men might question a talkative person like Applecore; someone who would exaggerate the Oak Falls mystery out of all proportion. To avoid this possibility, Louise spoke up quickly:

"Could we make a bargain with you?"

Bill McCaffrey laughed. "That all depends. What's the deal?"

"If we promise to give you the whole story when this mischief-maker is identified," she replied, "will you promise not to put anything in your paper now?"

The two reporters looked at each other and finally Joe Steele conceded, "That sounds reasonable. As a matter of fact, what we thought would be a bang-up ghost story seems to have petered out to nothing. So maybe this way we'll at least end up with *something*."

"Tell you what." Bill eyed the Danas shrewdly. "We'll give you girls one week to solve the mystery. If we don't hear from you by that time, we'll be back!"

"Fair enough." Jean gave a wry smile. "We'll try to meet our deadline."

The Danas and Mr. Pryor fervently hoped that the newsmen meant what they had promised. They thanked the reporters profusely and went with them onto the portico. As the two men started down the steps, the group suddenly was startled by strange sounds. They all stopped and listened incredulously.

"The—the stone tiger!" Bill McCaffrey exclaimed.

Hissing, snarling noises were issuing from the marble animal's throat!

CHAPTER XVI

"Secret Mission"

THE stone tiger was snarling like a real jungle beast! The Danas felt they must be dreaming. Mr. Pryor and the reporters stood transfixed with amazement until the unnerving sounds from the statue ceased.

The newsmen turned on the steps and looked squarely at Louise and Jean. "So your practical joker has left town, has he?" asked Joe Steele sarcastically. "Bill, it looks as if we have a story after all."

The Danas and Mr. Pryor were nonplused. A new dimension had been added to the mystery, giving the two reporters fresh material!

Bill McCaffrey strode over to the tiger and thrust his hand into its mouth. He pulled out a strange-looking gadget. The others hurried over and stared at the device which looked like a tiny music box.

"Apparently there's a record inside," Louise observed.

From the mechanism hung several wires with attached batteries and an automatic timer.

"Pretty clever, but evidently homemade," Joe remarked. "Mr. Pryor, what can you tell us about this?"

"Absolutely nothing," was the curator's mystified reply. "I never saw it before."

The Danas also insisted they knew nothing about the source of the device. "We're as much in the dark as you," Jean assured the reporters.

As Bill started to put the gadget into his pocket, Louise said firmly, "You can't take that! It should go to the police!"

"I suppose you're right," Bill McCaffrey conceded, and handed the box to Louise. "Be sure you do turn this over to them."

As the men again started to leave, Jean called after them, "Does our agreement about solving the mystery in a week still stand?"

The two reporters stopped and considered her question a moment. Finally they nodded and Joe said, "I've never been one to go back on my word."

As the men walked off, a look of relief came over Mr. Pryor's face and he thanked the girls profusely for their help. "I really wasn't sure what to say," he confessed. "What's your next step towards solving this mystery?"

Jean said she thought visiting electronic supply

stores in town might bring some clues to the maker of the gadget.

The girls told the curator about the strange telephone call received at the Dana home the previous night. Louise added, "Some of the sounds on the record in *this* gadget are exactly the same as those we heard on the phone."

The sisters left the puzzled curator and drove into the business centre. They stopped at one store after another. At none of them could the Danas pick up a single bit of evidence to prove that the maker of the little recording box had purchased his materials there. Finally Louise and Jean went to headquarters and turned in the gadget. They reported their fruitless inquiries.

"Too bad," commented the desk sergeant. "This fellow's clever—but he's bound to make a slip-up."

As the sisters left the police building, Jean said, "Where do we go from here? We seem to be stymied."

"Maybe not," Louise replied. "Why don't we go to Irving's automobile repair shop and question the owner? I still think Emil Gifford is mixed up in this mystery. He's a skilled mechanic and certainly could have put that sound box together without any difficulty."

"Good hunch, Louise," Jean praised her. "Emil might have inserted the box in the tiger's mouth during the night and set the timer to have the record play at various intervals. If he missed one audience, he would get another."

The girls drove up to the garage. Mr. Irving seemed surprised to see them. "Something go wrong with the car?" he asked at once.

Louise assured him that the automobile was working perfectly. "We've come on a different errand this time." She described the strange gadget found at the museum and asked if any parts for it could have come from his shop.

"Oh, yes," Mr. Irving answered. "In fact, some small auto parts have disappeared from here lately. The thief probably *could* have used them for that purpose."

Jean asked, "Did the thefts occur after Emil Gifford left?"

"Yes, and now that you bring up his name, I'll tell you I kind of suspect him."

Mr. Irving went on to say that it was quite possible Emil had had a duplicate key made for the shop door. "That man," the owner went on, "has an uncanny ability to repair or put together almost any kind of machinery."

Louise felt a tingle of excitement. At last perhaps the girls were finding a valuable lead! "Could Emil make a recorder?" she asked.

"He sure could," replied Mr. Irving. "To tell you the truth, Miss Dana, I wish Emil hadn't acted the way he did. He's almost a genius even if he is lazy. My business has slumped in just the short time since he left."

"Nobody seems to know where he or his wife went," Jean spoke up. "We thought we saw him in town, but he could be miles away by now."

The garage owner had surprising information of his own for the Danas. "I was talking to head-quarters a few minutes ago," he began. "The officer told me that they've located Emil's wife. She's staying with her folks in Florida. And here's a surprise for you. Mrs. Gifford told the police that Emil had said he was going away on some important business —a secret mission—and she wouldn't hear from him for a long while."

"This sure *is* news!" said Jean. "Of course, Emil could've come right back here after leaving his wife. His 'important business' may be some underhanded work in connection with the Oak Falls mystery."

Just then a car drove into the garage, so the Danas said good-bye to Mr. Irving and went home. Aunt Harriet greeted them with twinkling eyes and said:

"I'd like to bet you girls have forgotten you're going to a dance tonight."

"Oh dear, I had!" Louise exclaimed.

"Me too!" Jean admitted.

Miss Dana said that Ken and Chris had tele-phoned that they would arrive at five o'clock.

"Great!" cried Jean. "I hope the club is still having the dance—I'd better check."

She dashed to the phone to call Jane Humphrey.

To her relief Jane said, "Sure, the dance is on! All set?"

"Yes, and we're looking forward to it," Jean assured her friend. "Our dates will be here late this afternoon. Well, good-bye. See you tonight."

Aunt Harriet inquired of her nieces, "What are you going to wear?"

"Dresses that need pressing," Louise replied, grinning, "and I'd better look over my red coat with the high collar."

Jean had planned to wear a blue coat trimmed with a ruffled collar.

The sisters went upstairs and took their dance dresses from a closet. Jean gave a low giggle. "I'm going to do the pressing myself," she said, "even if Applecore offers. I want to be sure of wearing something that doesn't have a big scorched spot on it!"

Louise laughed and said she, too, would press her own dress. By the time the boys arrived in Ken's car, Jean and Louise, looking very attractive, were ready for their big evening. The plan was to have a light supper at the Dana home and to eat dinner at the party at ten o'clock.

"Hi!" the four young people greeted each other as they met in the hall.

"Long time, no see," Ken Scott said, grinning broadly.

He was a tall, slim youth with blond hair, whom Louise frequently dated. Christ Barton, dark-haired and full of fun, was a special friend of Jean's. The boys attended a prep school a short distance from Starhurst.

"We're glad you could make it," said Jean.

"How are the two prettiest detectives in the business?" Chris chuckled. "Bet you're on a new case!"

"Right!" Louise answered, her eyes sparkling. "The Dinner Dance Mystery!"

While enjoying supper the girls told Ken and Chris of the strange happenings in Oak Falls. The boys were intrigued. Soon afterwards, the young people were ready to leave for the dance.

"Good-bye," called Aunt Harriet. "Have a good time, but watch out for the black-robed ghost!" They promised, then set off.

The dance was being held at a country club on the outskirts of Oak Falls. When the Danas and their escorts arrived, the band was already playing, but it was some time before the two couples had a chance to dance. Friends of the girls, whom they had not seen in a long time, crowded around them in the lobby, eager to hear about the sisters' trip. Finally the four broke away and joined the dancers.

Tables for ten had been arranged around the edge of the floor. The Danas had invitations from various groups to join them. The sisters finally decided to sit with Jane Humphrey and her escort, and two other couples who had been childhood friends.

While the guests were eating, a group of the club

members put on a little variety show. The Danas were surprised to find that one of their friends had become an excellent singer. Another girl and her date did an intricate dance routine, and the final act was a clever pantomime by four of the club members. The applause was loud and there were several encores.

It was late when the dance ended and Louise, Jean, Chris, and Ken started for home. On the way, the girls told their escorts more about their recent sleuthing and the fact that they hoped to solve the mystery within a week.

"Wow!" Chris exclaimed. "What a challenge!"

"It is," Louise agreed. "Jean and I have one hunch—that the mystery centres around the stone tiger at the museum. Would you boys like to stop there?"

"We sure would," Chris replied.

Jean giggled. "If we sneak up very quietly, we might even be able to show you a ghost."

Ken grinned. "Lead me to him!"

Louise suggested that they leave the car on Snowden Drive beyond the Hilary cottage and make their way quietly through the grounds around the side of the museum to the statue. She laughed. "I only hope the police won't grab us!"

In a short while they parked, and the young people hopped out. As soon as their eyes became accustomed to the darkness, the foursome walked stealthily beside the hedge, tiptoed along the side of the museum, and turned the corner at the front. There they suddenly stopped and stared ahead in utter astonishment.

In the light of the moon and that streaming from the museum's hall windows, they could see a black-robed figure close to the stone tiger! *He was chipping at a claw of the beast!*

CHAPTER XVII

Smoke-Charm Magic

"STOP!" Jean cried frantically.

She dashed towards the black-robed figure mutilating the stone tiger. Louise, Ken, and Chris ran after her.

The mysterious person, alerted by Jean's outcry, fled in the opposite direction among some trees. As soon as he was out of the zone of light it was almost impossible to see him. His pursuers caught fleeting glimpses of the shrouded form as he dashed alongside the museum. Louise sighted the short man as he paused to fling off the long black robe.

"It's hampering his speed," she guessed.

Unburdened, the fugitive ran as fast as a deer and in a few moments vanished completely. The Danas and their friends gave up the chase and returned to the spot where the black robe lay. Ken picked it up, then the four young people went back to the front of the museum to look at it. The garment was of cheap black cloth and zipped up the front to the neck. There was a large hood attached, with a visor to cover the wearer's face.

"This outfit looks homemade," Louise remarked.

"Which could be a lead," Chris said with a chuckle. "Exhibit Number X for the police, I'll bet. How many clues have you discovered?"

The Danas laughed. "We've lost count," Jean answered. "Too bad he didn't leave the tool." The sisters were busy examining the claw of the tiger to see the damage. "I wish we had a flashlight."

Just then a patrol car arrived. Officers Brownell and Gibbs emerged and hurried up the path. They recognized the Dana girls, and seemed surprised to see them at the museum. Louise introduced Ken and Chris, then told what the four had just witnessed. She held out the black robe and hood.

The officers looked concerned. "We were here fifteen minutes ago," Officer Brownell remarked. "That mischief-maker is clever. He has our prowl-car schedule all figured out, even though we've changed it several times."

The policemen focused their flashlights on the tiger, revealing the deep gouges in the left front paw.

"It's a shame to think of anyone's hacking at this beautiful piece," Jean remarked indignantly.

The officers said they would request headquarters to station a guard on the estate grounds during the rest of the night. "But I don't think that ghost fellow will dare return," Officer Gibbs added.

The young people gave a description of the fugitive's height and build. The officers revealed that it tallied with those given by some citizens who had been frightened by the black-robed ghost.

The girls and their escorts said good night and drove home. The following morning they all went to church. After dinner the sisters asked the boys if they would like to go to the Hilary Museum and look around.

"Sure would," replied Ken. "Let's start!"

Mr. Pryor was delighted to see them, though upset about the previous night's episode. He gave Ken and Chris a personal tour of the museum.

"You boys interested in a challenge?" asked Jean.

They looked at her curiously.

"Suppose you try to find the hidden closet with the peephole. We'll give you one clue. You'll locate it from the landing of the main staircase."

Louise, Jean, and Mr. Pryor watched in amusement as the boys tried moving the wall panels. It was several minutes before they found the right combination. When they did, Ken and Chris grinned in satisfaction, as they revealed the hidden closet beyond. The boys soon detected the movable panel in the far wall and looked through the peephole into the large display room.

"This is ingenious!" Ken said.

Chris looked at the closet floor. Suddenly he stooped and exclaimed, "Hold everything! I've found a clue!"

He held up a man's soft slipper of the type worn by many people in India.

"That certainly *is* a good clue," said Mr. Pryor, taking the slipper. "But how and when did it get in there? The girls and I didn't see any slipper when we opened it before."

"Which means," Louise said worriedly, "that the mysterious intruder is getting into this place even when the windows and doors are locked! It's odd that he would leave one of his slippers."

She asked Mr. Pryor for a flashlight. When he brought it to her the young sleuth swept the closet with the bright beam. A look of excitement came into Louise's eyes as she peered at the ceiling. "There's a crack!" she exclaimed, reaching up. The next second she pushed aside a wide panel.

The others stared in astonishment. "Mr. Pryor, what's up above here?" Louise asked.

"I don't know," he confessed. "This whole closet is a revelation to me!" Ken offered to pull himself up and investigate the area above.

"You may come face to face with the person we're trying to find!" said Jean. "Do be careful!"

Ken took the light and managed to squeeze through the opening. In a moment he called down,

"There's a narrow flight of steps leading up to a small attic."

"Is there any exit from it to the roof?" Louise asked eagerly.

There was a short silence as Ken ascended the steps. He called down, "Yes, there is. A trap door leads to the roof!"

Mr. Pryor's mouth dropped open in astonishment. "So *this* is how the intruder has been sneaking in!" he said. "Well, he won't be able to from now on. I'll get a hammer and nails and fasten that trap door tight as a drum!"

He hurried downstairs as the girls and Chris climbed the hidden stairway to the attic to look at the trap door.

"If this is the way the intruder enters," said Louise, "he'd still have to get up on the roof. Let's see what we can find out."

The trap door was pushed open and the young people hoisted themselves onto the roof. It was flat in this section, so they could walk around easily.

"I think I've found the answer!" Jean cried out a moment later.

She pointed to a stout trellis that ran down the side of the building to the ground. In a niche of the mansion, and covered with vines and shaded by trees, it was quite inconspicuous.

"This must be the mystery man's ladder," said Ken.

The Danas and their friends climbed down and met Mr. Pryor returning with his tools. He was astounded to hear of the latest discovery. "Will you boys help me tear down that trellis?" he asked.

Ken and Chris were glad to be of assistance and seemed excited at continuing the detective work. First, the trap door in the ceiling was securely fastened. Next, the movable panel in the closet was nailed shut. Finally the trellis was torn down.

"Now maybe your troubles will be over," said Chris to Mr. Pryor.

"I wish I could believe it," the curator replied. "I cabled the maharajah for any information he could give us, but he is away on another trip." Mr. Pryor sighed. "None of our precautions in the museum will keep anyone from hacking at the stone tiger."

The Danas agreed with him. Unless, of course, thought the girls, a special watchman were put on constant guard near the statue. They did not mention this to Mr. Pryor, knowing that it would be a financial burden for the Hilarys.

"We'll just have to leave that worry for the police," they decided.

Ken glanced at his wristwatch and remarked that he and Chris must leave. They drove the Danas home, picked up their overnight bags, and thanked Aunt Harriet and the girls for their enjoyable visit. The young people waved good-bye, and the boys drove off.

Louise and Jean told their aunt about the trap door. Miss Dana was pleased. "I'm glad you all were able to batten down the hatches!" she said, in imitation of Uncle Ned. "By the way, the Hilarys would like us to come over as soon as possible. Also, I offered to have Cora help out at the cottage."

Jean grinned. "Well, what's keeping us?"

The three Danas packed their bags, then made sure every window and door was locked. They turned down the furnace thermostat and switched on upstairs and downstairs night lights. After a final check, Aunt Harriet and the girls drove off.

Elise welcomed the visitors warmly, and showed them to the comfortable room they would share. Then everyone gathered in Mrs. Hilary's quaintly decorated bedroom. The woman had brightened visibly upon seeing the Danas. In fact, she felt so much better she insisted upon going downstairs.

"We'll all have supper together," she declared cheerily.

Her daughter smiled. "This is wonderful, Mother."

Elise built a fire in the living-room grate, and after supper they all sat around the fireplace, talking. Aunt Harriet and the girls were careful not to bring up any subject disturbing to Mrs. Hilary. By the end of the evening there was colour in her face and a sparkle in her eyes, which Elise later confided to Louise and Jean she had not seen since her father's death.

"I'm so grateful to you. But please don't feel you have to stay in the house all the time—come and go just as you please, and by all means don't abandon the mystery!"

Louise and Jean reminded her in low tones that they had less than a week to solve the mystery. Otherwise, the story might break in all the newspapers. Elise became grave, realizing that if written up distastefully, this might damage the image of lovely old Oak Falls, and the Hilarys and their museum.

Suddenly Jean began to sniff. "What do I smell?" she asked. "It's like—like burning oil."

"The cottage has a gas-fired furnace, so it couldn't be coming from anywhere in here," said Elise. "The wind must be carrying the odour here from some distance."

Soon everyone became drowsy and decided to retire. The next morning, as Jean and Louise finished dressing, they heard a shriek of fear just outside the front door. Louise and Jean dashed to a window and looked down.

Cora Appel stood on the path leading to the porch of the cottage. She wore a winter coat and a fur hat that was askew. A scarf tied around her neck was about to fall off and she had dropped the handbag she was carrying. She was staring down at the pavement, a horrified expression on her face. "Oh, I can't stand it! I just can't work here!" Cora wailed loudly.

From where Louise and Jean stood they could not see what had startled the maid. The girls rushed out into the hall and down the stairway. They were joined by Elise, who had also heard the outcry. Together, the girls raced outdoors to where Cora was standing.

Seeing them, she exclaimed, "Look! The ghost again!"

Chalked on the stone path was a strange symbolic-looking set of lines and curves that crossed and crisscrossed. They formed a double triangle with an oval in the centre. Each boxed section contained a number. Around the periphery were arrows—some pointing towards, and some away from the figures—and patches of squares, like a tick-tack-toe game.

To one side of the design lay a small heap of ashes which the Danas guessed was probably from burned oil-soaked rags and paper. "Perhaps this is what we smelled last night," Louise said.

Elise was gazing at the design in fascination. "That's a smoke charm!" she said excitedly. "But it's not a threat—it's a wish for recovery from illness."

This announcement calmed Cora. "You mean it was put there on account of your mother's being sick?"

"I believe so," Elise replied. "But I can't imagine who left it here."

Cora, feeling reassured, went on into the house,

where Aunt Harriet gave her some chores. Meanwhile, the three girls continued to study the charm.

"In India," Elise explained, "superstitious natives still believe that magicians can cure disease, and use a method similar to this one.

"It's done with an elaborate ceremony," she went on. "Part of it consists of drawing the charm, usually on the lid of a new earthen pot, and its design is made with grey ashes.

"A small vessel containing oil is placed on top of the lid and the oil is lighted. While it's burning, the magician touches the patient on the painful part of his body and singsongs an incantation."

Louise had been listening intently. Now she said, "If this is a friendly gesture, it seems pretty certain that Mr. Abdul didn't leave the charm. Elise, have you any Indian friends in this country who are superstitious and might have drawn this?"

Elise shook her head. "This is a complete mystery to me. If I do have an Indian friend in this country, I wish he or she would come here. He might help solve the problem of the stone tiger."

Jean had been scrutinizing the ground, looking for a clue to the person who had drawn the smoke charm. Presently she picked up a small piece of white chalk.

"This looks like plain old American chalk, but it may lead us to some sort of helpful information. Louise, right after breakfast, let's go into town and find out if anybody from India has bought chalk lately. It's a long shot, but worth trying."

Her sister agreed. Within an hour the two girls set off for the business section of Oak Falls in great anticipation. Each wondered if the trip would shed some light on the mystery.

CHAPTER XVIII

Puzzle in Numbers

AFTER Louise and Jean had inquired at the shops in Oak Falls which sold chalk, they wearily admitted that their sleuthing had been in vain. The girls turned towards the Hilary cottage, but presently Louise stopped.

"I think," she said, "we should let Sergeant Renley know where we're staying."

"And maybe he has news for us," Jean said hopefully.

The sergeant happened to be at headquarters and was glad to see them. He praised the girls for their various reports and the evidence which they had provided.

"Our lab has been analyzing the black gown," the officer told them, "but nothing distinctive about it has been found yet. The only thing of interest I can tell you is that we took the outfit to the Mc-

Gregor farm to have their pet Mickey smell it. From the dog's growls and excited response I'd say the robe must belong to the man who borrowed him."

"Any news about the tiger?" Louise asked.

"None. And no word yet on Emil Gifford. We think maybe he is holed up somewhere," Sergeant Renley said.

Jean told the officer about the smoke charm on the Hilary path. "It was drawn with this chalk," she added, taking the piece from her pocket. "Are you interested in keeping it?" Smiling, she handed the chalk to him.

The sergeant nodded, although he doubted it would be of much help. "But as you girls well know, a good detective *never* turns down the smallest bit of evidence."

Sergeant Renley also emphasized his great interest in Jean's explanation of the charm.

"I must admit," he said, "I've never heard of a smoke charm before. But you say it is meant for a *good* omen, which doesn't fit into the picture of our suspect with all his threats and warnings."

Unable to learn anything more at headquarters, Louise and Jean left. "Let's stop at our house for the mail," Louise suggested.

Just as they unlocked the front door to their home, the telephone began to ring. Louise dashed to answer it. "Uncle Ned!" she whispered to Jean.

"Hilarys' line was busy," he said, "so tried

reaching you here. Mystery solved yet? . . . No? . . . I'm talking to you from shipboard, so I must be brief. Listen carefully. I checked with an official at the Immigration Service about recent visitors from India to our part of the state. I also learned this—a man named Rasalu and a couple, Lona and Baghtu Surat, are in this country now. But there was no Mr. Abdul on the list. I must go now, me hearties. Keep well. Lots of luck. Goodbye."

Louise relayed the full message to her sister and wrote down the names Rasalu, and Lona and Baghtu Surat. She ended by saying, "Jean, do you think one of those two men could be posing as Mr. Abdul?"

"Could be," her sister remarked. "Let's ask Elise and her mother if they know these people."

Neither of the Hilarys had heard of the man Rasalu, but both exclaimed in amazement upon hearing the name Surat.

"Lona was my *amah* when I was a little girl," said Elise. "That means nurse."

"She was a lovely person," Mrs. Hilary added. "I always felt perfectly safe leaving Elise alone with her."

Louise asked how recently the Hilarys had seen Lona. "Oh, not for a long time," Elise's mother replied. "You see, we returned to this country to live many years ago, then went back several times to India, but not where Lona was."

Jean asked, "Is Baghtu Lona's husband?"

"Yes," Elise said. "He has been a servant of my father's friend the maharajah for many years. After we came back here the first time, Lona also went to work for him. But I'm surprised to hear of the Surats' being in this country. I hope they'll come to see us."

"I do too," Mrs. Hilary said wistfully.

All this time Louise had been wondering whether the Surats actually might be in Oak Falls. Perhaps they had left the smoke charm! Finally she broached the subject to the Hilarys.

Mrs. Hilary's eyes lighted up. "Possibly. Lona and her husband were steeped in the ancient superstitions of their country."

Aunt Harriet, who had been listening but taking no part in the conversation, now spoke up. "Virginia, you look so much better and seem much more like your old self. I believe that smoke charm has worked its magic!"

Mrs. Hilary laughed. "I also believe your good company has given me a real lift."

Louise asked Jean and Elise to go outside and study the smoke charm with her. The three girls knelt down on the front path and gazed at the outline. It contained the number 11 at the top, then 4, 22, and 12. Below this, left to right, were 19 and 18; centred under them was the number 16. At the very bottom, on the left, was 14, and 48 on the right.

Suddenly Louise bent way down and stared at the quadrangular section in the centre containing the number 12. Under this had been printed faintly the name *Hilary*.

"This definitely was meant for either you or your mother," Louise exclaimed to Elise.

"And the 48! That's the number of your house!" Jean cried out.

By this time Elise's brow was furrowed as she concentrated on the puzzle. Suddenly she said, "I think I have part of it! That 4 could stand for the fourth month, April, in which my mother was born. The 19, her actual birth date—the 22 her age when married, and 18 is the date of my parents' wedding anniversary."

"Wonderful!" said Louise, giving her friend a little hug. "Now tell us what the 11, 12, 16, and 14 stand for."

Elise stared at these numbers for several seconds. "I can't figure them out," she replied. "And those other symbols don't mean a thing to me. Well," she added, getting up, "I'll keep on cudgeling my brain, and if any new idea pops into it, I'll let you know."

The rest of the day went by without Elise or her mother being able to figure out the odd symbols. After supper Cora asked the girls if they would accompany her home.

"Of course," said Louise. "It's such a beautiful evening—let's walk."

Elise offered to go along, so the four set off across

town. The air was crisp and everyone kept a fast pace.

Cora shivered. "Sure glad you all came with me. It's awful dark tonight—hardly any stars."

On the way back, Jean said to Louise and Elise, "I have a hunch that stone-tiger chipper will be back. I'm beginning to think he didn't find what he was looking for in the museum, so he hopes it's inside the tiger. He doesn't know the statue is solid."

"Elise," said Louise with a chuckle, "I can guess what Jean is leading up to. She's eager for us to do some spy work—namely, see if that same fellow shows up with his chipping tool tonight."

"That's a marvellous idea," Elise replied. "Shall we go right now?"

"Sure!"

The three girls entered the Hilary grounds from Snowden Drive. They tiptoed along in the darkness and took up their posts behind bushes at the front corner of the building.

"Listen!" Louise whispered.

The girls could hear muffled pounding sounds and peered cautiously around. Now they noticed that the front of the museum was in darkness. The trio wondered whether Mr. Pryor had forgotten to leave the hall light on, or whether it had been turned off by someone else.

At that moment a squad car pulled up at the curb and two policemen jumped out, beaming flashlights ahead as they approached.

"Let's hide!" said Louise. "If somebody is working on the tiger, we don't want him to know we're around."

The girls hastily flattened themselves on the ground behind the bushes. The policemen's flashlights did not reveal the girls, or disclose anyone else as they tried the doors. If an intruder had been near the statue, he must have escaped unnoticed.

Within five minutes the police had driven away. Soundlessly the girls stood up and listened. Soon afterwards, they heard the same muffled noise!

Jean grabbed Louise and Elise and urged them forward. Not a word was said as they silently crept towards the stone tiger. Even in the darkness they could make out a black-robed figure at work on the statue!

Again Jean signalled her companions and together they leaped to the man's side. The next instant the three girls pounced on the ghost, knocking him down!

CHAPTER XIX

Trapped Underground

As THE three girls held down the struggling black-robed figure, Louise tore the mask from his face.

"Emil Gifford!" she cried out.

The captive's response electrified them. In a clipped British accent he rasped, "Ah—what? I'm a tiger! Let me go or I will claw you to pieces!"

Louise, Jean, and Elise let Emil stand up but held on to him firmly. He tried to wrench himself from their grasp but his efforts were futile.

"So you're the mysterious person who has been scaring Oak Falls half to death," Jean said angrily.

"I do not know what you are talking about," Emil replied stiffly. "I have done nothing I was not told to do."

"Who told you to do what?" Louise demanded.

The mechanic said, "My master is Abdul. He is a great man and performs miracles. He has promised me riches if I will be a tiger."

By now the Danas wondered whether Emil's speech and his mind had been affected by his apparent association with the mysterious Mr. Abdul. His behaviour was that of a person under the influence of hypnotism.

"Why did Mr. Abdul want you to be a tiger?" Jean asked calmly.

Emil Gifford gave a hollow laugh. "To scare people away from the woods. They belong to Mr. Abdul and me. No one can take them away from us!"

"So you were playing tiger over there?" Jean quizzed their prisoner.

Emil Gifford nodded. "But what right have you to question me?"

Louise laughed. "You know us, Emil—and you know why we're asking."

"I never saw any of you before in my life," the mechanic said stubbornly.

Suddenly his eyes fastened on the stone tiger. In a high, faraway voice, he chanted, "Ancient ivory —priceless gifts—ghost—black veins—"

"Maybe," Louise whispered to her sister, "his mind really *has* snapped."

Jean was still suspicious. She was sure Emil Gifford was putting on an act. He was apparently a cohort of the strange Mr. Abdul, and now was trying to put all the blame on him. Had each of them worn a black robe, and alternated in chipping the stone tiger? Yet, the dog Mickey had found Mr.

Abdul's scent on the discarded garment. The Danas figured Emil had borrowed it the previous evening.

By tacit agreement the three girls guided their prisoner along the path which led to the Hilary cottage. He kept mumbling strange, incoherent phrases, none of which seemed to relate to the mystery. To their amazement, Emil did not seem to have any desire to break away. The girls decided to stand guard over him and notify the police.

"Why were you chipping the stone tiger?" Louise asked.

"I don't know. Mr. Abdul told me to."

"Where did you hide when the police came a while ago?" she pressed.

"Oh, I know secret places around here," was the noncommittal answer, but he did not explain. When the girls walked into the Hilary house with Emil Gifford, Louise introduced him, giving Aunt Harriet and Mrs. Hilary a warning wink.

The women realized at once that something unusual was going on, but waited for the girls to do the talking. Emil Gifford's irrational replies to their questions confirmed their theory that he was under some kind of spell. Jean went to the upstairs telephone and called Sergeant Renley at his home.

"You girls have caught the ghost?" the officer asked unbelievingly. "Well, you deserve a police honour medal."

Jean laughed. "We'll accept it *after* we catch Mr. Abdul," she responded.

The sergeant arrived with Officer Gibbs shortly. Emil Gifford looked at them stupefied. "Why are you police here?" he asked.

"Because a lot of people have been asking us to look for you," Sergeant Renley answered. "One of them is your wife."

"Oh, I'll be seeing her," Emil said without enthusiasm. "I got a job to do first. I am—"

Suddenly he ceased speaking and refused to answer any further questions. Out of earshot of the prisoner, Louise told the officers about Emil's strange actions.

"We'll have our psychiatrist talk with him," the sergeant promised.

After the police had taken Emil away, Louise telephoned Mr. Pryor. He came over at once and was aghast upon learning the latest news about the mutilation to the stone tiger.

"This settles it!" he said. "There's no money to engage a night guard, but I'll act as one myself until this mystery is completely solved!"

"But if you're on duty all day," Mrs. Hilary objected, "you'll need to rest at night."

No amount of persuasion would deter Mr. Pryor from his resolve. The curator announced he would immediately station himself near the statue for the remainder of the night.

"If, by chance, I do fall asleep," he added, "and anyone starts chipping, the noise will certainly wake me up!"

"But if you're asleep, the person may harm you!" Mrs. Hilary said worriedly.

"I'll hide behind some bushes," the curator assured her. Then, without further delay, he left to take up his new duty.

While the Danas were getting ready for bed, Louise said to her sister, "If Emil was masquerading as the tiger, that means the woods are safe now. Tomorrow morning let's go out there again and look around. We might even find Mr. Abdul's hiding place!"

At breakfast the Danas told their plan to the others and invited Elise to go with them.

"Are you sure you'll be all right?" Mrs. Hilary asked apprehensively.

"Three of us together will be safe," her daughter said reassuringly.

Louise drove silently to the area. She parked and they started their trek. The path seemed more trampled than it had on their previous search.

"It looks as if several people have been here lately," Jean remarked.

They passed the tree where the chipping tool had been found and kept on, proceeding cautiously.

Presently Elise looked up. "Snowflakes," she noted. "We'd better hurry so we won't get caught in a storm."

The girls had walked about a quarter mile into the woods without seeing a cabin or any place where a person could hide. A short distance ahead

Jean spotted a small pile of logs. It was well screened by trees and bushes.

"This is a funny place to stack logs," she commented, and the others agreed.

The three searchers left the path to examine the logs. They rolled a couple aside, and were startled to see a flat wooden door beneath. Quickly they tossed aside the rest of the logs. The door, flush to the ground, was securely bolted with a long wooden bar.

"Could this be Mr. Abdul's hiding place?" Elise whispered.

Louise shrugged and said she thought it was the opening to a cellar. "Probably a house once stood here and this was sort of an outside cold cellar. Let's look inside."

Jean quickly yanked out the wooden bar. As the girls started to lift the heavy door, they heard a muffled cry from below.

Elise stiffened. "That's the Indian call for help!" she said excitedly.

Together, Jean and Louise flung the door wide. Leading downward were stone steps. Hearts pounding, the three girls descended into what seemed to be a cellar. A moment later they stepped back in shocked dismay.

Two prisoners, a man and a woman, securely tied and their heads covered, lay face down on the floor!

As the girls dashed forward to release them, the

heavy door above slammed shut. They could hear the big bolt being fastened into place.

"Oh!" Louise cried out. "How stupid of us not to have left a guard outside. Now *we're* prisoners too!"

The girls, in total darkness, could hear the logs being piled over the door. It flashed through the Danas' minds that even though rescuers did search the woods, they might never guess the logs to be a camouflage, and pass right by the spot!

At that moment a menacing voice, with a British accent, came clearly to them from above:

"Miss Hilary, and your friends the Dana girls— I will cast a spell over all you meddlers until I accomplish my mission here! Meanwhile, you will remain my captives!"

CHAPTER XX

Escape!

THE girls, stunned and angry, stood in the total darkness of their underground prison. The captive man began to speak in a tongue unfamiliar to the Danas.

"It's an Indian dialect," Elise whispered, then translated, "He says there's a flashlight somewhere in this cellar."

Instantly the girls got down on hands and knees and began to feel around the earthen floor. Presently Louise's fingers touched the flashlight in a corner and she snapped it on. The bright beam revealed the prisoners clearly. Their heads and faces were completely covered with silk scarves tied at the back of the neck. The rescuers untied the scarves and rolled the couple over on their backs.

Elise gave a little scream of astonishment. "Lona! Baghtu!" she cried out.

The Danas stared in amazement as their friend

excitedly began speaking in the Indian dialect with the man and woman. Both had fine features, dark-brown eyes, and shining black hair. The girls released the prisoners, who stood up and exercised their cramped limbs.

"They are Lona and Baghtu Surat," Elise told the Danas. "You remember that Lona was my *amah* when I was a little girl?"

The sisters nodded, eager to hear the couple's story. They waited fully ten minutes before Elise translated it, explaining that the Surats spoke very little English.

"Back in India," she began, "Lona and Baghtu worked for the maharajah at the time he sent the stone tiger to my father. It seems that secretly the maharajah was also sending some very old and extremely valuable ivory figurines for the museum. He did not tell anyone except my father how these were being sent, since some of his treasures had been stolen. It was all right to send the figurines that way, because there is no import duty on antiques. Then the maharajah went hunting and did not hear of my father's death.

"In the meantime, another servant in the maharajah's palace—a man named Rasalu—learned about the shipment. When he heard of my father's death, Rasalu determined to come to America and steal the collection, which Baghtu says is worth a fortune.

"Lona and Baghtu, always loyal to my family,

decided to follow Rasalu to this country. When they arrived in Oak Falls they heard of the strange happenings in town and decided it was the work of Rasalu. He fancies himself to be quite a soothsayer, magician, and hypnotist. Lona thinks he is just a crazy egotist.

"Being in town has been embarrassing for the Surats. The police questioned them, but finally were satisfied with their credentials. I guess that's why Sergeant Renley didn't tell us about them. Lona says they asked her husband if he went under the name of Mr. Abdul. Finally Lona and Baghtu decided that Rasalu must be the one using that name.

"The Surats wanted to contact Mother and me," Elise went on, "but when they learned that Rasalu was causing trouble for us, they decided to try capturing Rasalu first. They did, however, leave the smoke charm, hoping it would make Mother feel better."

Jean interrupted to ask what the other numbers on the charm meant. Elise queried Lona, who said they were based on an old legend in Lona's family and signified a wish for health and happiness.

Elise continued:

"Lona and Baghtu were becoming desperate because they could not find Rasalu. They were fearful he might have already disappeared with the ivory figurines. Then, quite by accident, they learned from a waitress at a restaurant in town that

Mr. Abdul had gone to New York but would be back. Lona and Baghtu practically camped at the airport, scrutinizing each incoming passenger.

"Finally they were rewarded. Sunday night a man wearing a grey wig and moustache came through the terminal building. Lona and Baghtu recognized him—Rasalu in disguise! They accused him of scheming to steal the ivory figurines—if he had not already done so.

"Rasalu admitted he was hunting for the treasure, but assured the couple he had not yet found it. To Lona and Baghtu's surprise, he invited them to have dinner in town with him and he would tell them everything.

"Unfortunately, they believed him. When he suggested stopping first for coffee at the airport lunch counter, they agreed. Then they all went out to his car. Suddenly Lona and Baghtu became very sleepy. They awoke to find themselves tied up in this cellar.

"To their amazement, they could now remember certain details of the trip from the airport, for instance that Rasalu had marched them a long distance through the woods. On the way they had met a man he called Emil. Rasalu had ordered Emil to get busy with the chipping tool and be sure to wear his black robe.

"The Surats also remembered being guided into this cellar by a flashlight which Rasalu had turned off and laid down, once they were inside. Perhaps he heard some person or animal coming. In any case, he left the cellar, locked the door, and piled the logs on top."

"Just as they are now!" said Louise. "Well, Lona and Baghtu's story corroborates a lot of our suspicions. We must get out of here and help the police capture Rasalu!"

"But how?" Elise asked dubiously.

Louise and Jean were not to be discouraged and insisted they could smash the door open. They had observed that Baghtu was very muscular, and despite the ordeal he had been through, could probably be of great assistance. Elise translated the plan, and Baghtu replied that he would do his best.

The five prisoners ascended the steps of the wide opening and pushed with all their might, using their arms and shoulders. Suddenly they heard a cracking noise.

"It's beginning to give!" cried Jean.

Her optimism gave the weary captives renewed strength, and within five minutes they were able to wrench the bolt loose and raise one corner of the door enough for Louise to squeeze through. Quickly she tossed away the remaining logs. The other captives emerged and took deep lungsful of fresh air.

"We're free!" Elise exclaimed. She turned to her former *amah* and Baghtu, and the three, between laughs and tears, spoke rapidly in the Indian dialect. Then Elise turned to the Danas.

"Lona and Baghtu can't thank you both enough. Now let's all go to my home for a good meal."

"We'll call the police first thing," said Jean, "and put them on Rasalu's trail."

Luckily, only an inch of snow had fallen. Soon the group reached the Hilary cottage.

Elise's mother was amazed and overjoyed to see the Surats. While the four were talking excitedly, the Danas excused themselves and went upstairs. While Jean gave Aunt Harriet the full story, Louise telephoned Sergeant Renley. He was almost speechless at the news and could not praise the girls highly enough.

"We'll put a dragnet out at once for Rasalu," the sergeant declared. "This time we'll catch him for sure! By the way, Emil Gifford is out of his hypnotic state, and quite rational now, but he won't talk about the mystery."

The officer's prediction about Rasalu came true —he was captured the next day near the secret cellar and Sergeant Renley asked the Danas, Elise, and the Surats to come to headquarters.

Rasalu, about fifty years old, was tall and slender. There was hatred in his piercing black eyes as he glared at the visitors. The prisoner protested his innocence, but the Danas' evidence, combined with that of Lona and Baghtu, was so strong that he finally broke down.

The self-styled sorcerer confessed that he had thought people in Oak Falls would be as superstitious as some in India, and could be frightened off the streets at night.

Rasalu, therefore, had planned the ghost act, hoping to keep most of the residents at home, so that his treks between the woods, the recluse's house where he boarded, and the museum would be undetected. Also, it was less likely that he would be disturbed in his search of the museum, which he never gave up entirely. The Indian was responsible for putting the mask in the Danas' window, and leaving the turban and snake, and writing the notes to scare them off the case.

Cora's gossiping around town had alerted Rasalu to the sleuthing ability of Louise and Jean. Desperate when the Danas were not discouraged, he had started to carry Jean off one night to give them a good scare, and later buried the wax heads in the backyard. The Indian had phoned the Dana home and imitated the wild-animal sounds before giving the warning message.

Rasalu admitted arranging the dog attack, playing the eerie flute music, and throwing the mongoose at Louise. On his next visit to the museum when he tried to retrieve his ring, he stumbled on the top step of the hidden stairway. One of his slippers fell to the bottom. Rasalu thought he heard footsteps on the third floor and was afraid that whoever it was might go up to the attic and he would be caught, so he didn't dare go back for the lost slipper.

"But nothing would deter your persistence," he

said angrily. "The disgrace of being hounded by two girl detectives is unbearable!"

The Danas smiled and Louise asked, "What is your connection with Emil Gifford?"

Rasalu said he had met Emil, and finding him gullible, knew he would be an excellent hypnotic subject. When Rasalu did not succeed completely with this method of influencing Emil, he had put a drug he always carried into Emil's food. It was the same kind of pill which he had slipped into the Surats' coffee.

"I even taught Emil to speak as I do," Rasalu bragged. "From your local airport he pretended to phone me in New York, where I went to borrow money. Under hypnosis he sounded like my twin. I had him follow the Danas and use this trick to make them think I was still in Oak Falls."

Rasalu had had two robes made for him and Emil by the recluse's sister. They were black, so the wearer would not be seen until he jumped out at his victims. Rasalu and Emil had taken turns playing "ghost." They had, as suspected, managed to elude the police by figuring out about when the cruising patrol cars would stop at various points.

Through Emil's grandfather, a former caretaker of the old mansion, the mechanic had learned of the trellis, the secret entrance to the roof, and the hidden closet with the peephole. Rasalu, not wanting to climb the lattice, had ordered Emil to go with Mrs. Gifford to the museum, and, while she entered, to unlatch the front door. Rasalu had gained admittance several times before the Danas discovered the unlocked door.

After investigating every likely hiding place in the museum for the valuable ivory figurines, Rasalu had decided that the only possibility left was the stone tiger. Like Mr. Pryor, Rasalu had believed the statue was solid. But one day he remembered having heard the maharajah say:

"If you touch a white tiger's foot, you may meet sudden fortune."

Rasalu and Emil had taken turns chipping the tiger's claw. Emil had worn "his master's" robe the night of the dance. But enough of Rasalu's scent had been left on it for the dog Mickey to pick up. The Indian, sullen-faced, was led away.

A guard now brought in Emil Gifford. Learning that Rasalu had confessed, the mechanic talked freely in his natural voice. He admitted tampering with the Dana car so the accident would happen. Emil had figured that if the girls were injured and frightened, and their automobile badly damaged, they would not attempt to solve the Oak Falls mystery.

"But nothing scared you."

The mechanic had ingeniously made the tiger's eyes glow by using a chemical, and had built the midget record player which the newspaper reporters had found in the beast's mouth.

"But I wish I'd never met that Indian fakir!"

Emil sobbed. "I told him everything I knew myself and what I learned from Cora's gossiping. We even thought you might be hiding the ivory for the Hilarys and tried to get in your house one night on a ladder to search for it." Emil laughed mirthlessly. "Abdul tried to injure Louise with the mongoose and scare you away from the museum, but it didn't work. Sometimes he wasn't so smart. Once when we met to make plans, he stuck his chipping tool in a tree trunk while we were talking. He forgot to take it out. When he went back for it, the tool was gone. I told him about the cellar in the woods—my grandfather had a cabin there at one time. Sometimes Abdul kept his magician's things and the tiger suit in the cellar." Having completed his confession, Emil Gifford was led back to his cell.

When Mrs. Hilary heard the whole story, she was amazed and remarked, "It's hard to believe that any gift but the tiger was sent to my husband. And now that the mystery is solved, perhaps more people will be attracted to the museum and our financial worries will be over."

The widow seemed so happy that Louise and Jean did not hint they felt the mystery was far from being solved. They asked Elise if she would walk to the museum with them to tell Mr. Pryor the news of Rasalu's capture.

She willingly went along. On the way, Louise

asked, "Elise, do you think your mother would mind if *we* do a little chipping on the stone tiger to see if Rasalu's hunch is right?"

"After all," Jean added, "the Surats seem certain the maharajah *did* send the valuable ivory."

Elise did not reply at once. Finally she asked, "Do you think it could be done without mutilating the statue any more?"

"Mr. Pryor might know a way," Jean suggested to her.

The curator was overwhelmed by the news. He agreed to get the museum's chipping tool and work on the tiger, sure he could do so with little damage to the statue.

Since Mr. Pryor seemed uncertain where to start, Louise remarked, "Perhaps Emil unwittingly gave us a clue. He mentioned black veins. Do you suppose one of these black stripes hides something of value?"

Jean was excited by the idea. "And remember that reference to the tiger's foot? Maybe we should examine all these black stripes in the marble near the paws!"

Just then Keith Bartlett came across the grounds. He was grinning and looked so happy that the Danas felt sure he was bursting to tell them all something important.

Before he had a chance to speak, Elise rushed up and told him all that had happened during the past few hours and what Mr. Pryor and the girls were about to do. Intrigued, Keith watched in fascination.

After a careful examination of the tiger's four legs, Mr. Pryor decided to follow an observation that Jean had made—that two veins between the claw and right foreleg of the stone tiger, being wider and less wavy than the others, might be the key. Carefully Mr. Pryor wedged his sculptor's chipping tool alongside one stripe.

"This goes down more easily than I expected," he said excitedly.

The curator proceeded with extreme caution, but at last he called out, "It's coming!"

In a few seconds he lifted out a six-inch-long section of the black-and-white marble. Everyone stared into the two-inch crevice.

"Why, there's nothing inside!" said Elise in disappointment.

"I'll chip through the stone below," Mr. Pryor announced, "to see if there is a hollow place beneath." This time he tapped the tool with a small hammer.

The others watched tensely. Suddenly the curator exclaimed, "I've broken through! There *is* a hollow space. It must have been purposely done when the tiger was sculptured!"

Breathless with excitement, the Danas and their friends watched as Mr. Pryor thrust his long fingers into the opening. A second later his face broke into a wide smile. He withdrew his hand. In the palm of it was an exquisite ivory figurine of a Chinese woman. It was so delicately carved and so perfect in symmetry that everyone exclaimed in admiration.

"That is the most beautiful piece I've ever seen!" Elise cried. "Small, but every detail stands out."

"It's marvellous—simply marvellous!" said Louise, and Jean added, "Absolutely super!"

By this time Mr. Pryor had reached inside the tiger's leg and drawn out an equally lovely carving. Within a few moments the ebony base on which the stone creature stood was decorated with twelve of the priceless ivory figurines. There were Oriental rulers, peasants, dancers, and several animals.

As Mr. Pryor began to replace the chipped-out marble and insert the removed section in its proper groove, he said, "This is a happy day indeed!"

"It's especially happy for Elise and me," said Keith Bartlett, looking at her fondly. "I've been saving some big news of my own. You're looking at the new owner of the *Oak Falls News!*"

"Oh, Keith!" his fiancée exclaimed joyfully and threw her arms about him. "What happened?"

Elise and the Danas learned that Mr. Archer, who was well again, had called Keith in and admitted that he finally realized he was the right person to carry on the newspaper. After a final talk with Mr. Homer and Mr. Semple, the owner concluded their editorial policies would indeed make it cheap and sensational.

Keith had attended the conference and the two syndicate men had confessed to conniving with an Indian named Mr. Abdul, who claimed to be an astrologer. He had agreed to help them prepare the note to Elise which warned her not to marry Keith, but would throw suspicion away from them as the senders.

"They knew she would understand its significance, and hoped she would break our engagement. If this had happened, I might have left town and not bought the paper." Keith smiled. "But what they didn't know was that Elise is not superstitious, and they didn't realize how very much Elise and I mean to each other."

As the group walked to the Hilary cottage, carrying the figurines, there was loud praise of the Danas for solving the mystery.

"People will come from everywhere to visit Dad's museum and see this ivory," Elise predicted.

At the celebration dinner that evening in the Hilary home Elise looked unusually pretty and happy. Presently she stood up to speak. From a package she had previously concealed, Elise brought out two matching gold bracelets. Each was set with a beautiful ruby.

"Louise and Jean," she said, "these good-luck amulets belong to Mother and me. We bought them in India some time ago. But now we'd like you to have them, in appreciation for all you have done." Mrs. Hilary then presented Aunt Harriet with a richly decorated silk scarf.

All the Danas beamed and expressed their thanks for the gifts. Aunt Harriet was thinking, "I'm sure another mystery will come their way soon." And it did in **THE RIDDLE OF THE FROZEN FOUNTAIN.**

Louise's eyes twinkled as she asked those at the Hilary table, "Anybody here have a flute? I'd like to give you a little snake-charming music—Oak Falls style!"

"Better not try." Jean giggled. "You might be a target again for a mongoose!"

Oh, no!" moaned Cora, almost dropping the water pitcher from which she was filling glasses.

As everyone laughed, Elise said, "There's one more thing I want to show you, Louise and Jean." She took Jean's new bracelet, and with her thumbnail raised the ruby to reveal a tiny space beneath.

"See what's inside?" Elise said. "An authentic Indian charm and a memento of this case in which you outwitted the tiger—a tiny replica of a tiger's claw and some real tiger's whiskers!"